U0152296

CANTONESE

FOR

EVERYONE

—

REVISED

AND

ENLARGED

EDITION

—

H. R. WELLS

英粵通語

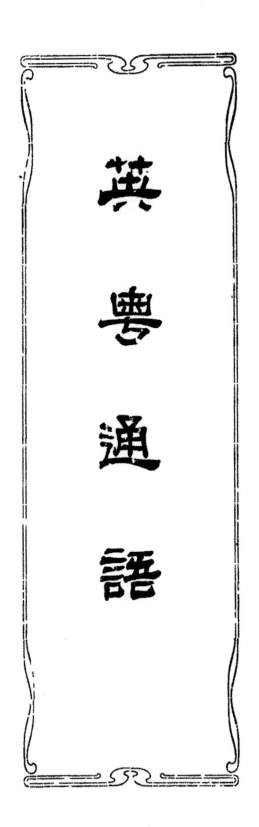

英粵通語

香港・澳門雙城成長經典

CANTONESE FOR EVERYONE

The Reverend H. R. WELLS, O.B.E.
London Mission,
Hong Kong.

Member of the Board of Examiners,
Hong Kong, for thirty years.
Director of Cantonese Class in
Hong Kong University for four years.

REVISED AND ENLARGED
EDITION

Printed by
KAE SHEAN PRINTING CO.,
59, Queen's Road Central
HONGKONG
1931.

INTRODUCTION.

This book is prepared to meet the needs of students wishing to get a fairly good command of Cantonese in a short time.

It must be learnt and used at the same time. Students should begin to talk from the start, a conversation is given after the first lesson, and may be used at once. Do not try to get a good vocabulary before beginning to speak.

It is better to employ a teacher, or join a class at first, but many can learn without this, if they really study, and practise the words.

When one has learnt the first ten lessons he has got material for constant use, and can go right forward. The first twenty lessons contain the key words to Cantonese, and sentences of all kinds are built on these words in the lessons and exercises.

The numbers will be found at the heads of the lessons, and lists of terminating words and classifiers, and a small extra vocabulary are printed on a separate sheet.

A table of tones or inflections is given, students should get some one to help them to understand these inflections.

Every word has its own inflection or tone, but some have also a changed tone, which is often indicated by an asterisk. A great many of the changed tones are rising inflections and are like the second high tone, a similar rising inflection is used in words of the fourth tone, which all end in k, p, or t, Paak₄ white is duplicated as *Paak₄ Paak₄, meaning " very white " and Paak₄ *Paak₄,—meaning " in vain."

The tones are in the natural pitch of one's voice, the high tones need not crack one's voice, nor the low tones become a growl.

It is necessary to get the correct inflection, as the wrong one means something else. Most people with practice and care can do quite well.

The tones are called First, second, third, and fourth high and low tones thus makes 8, and the middle fourth makes the ninth.

In Chinese the tones in the higher series, are called Sheung₃ P'ing₁ (even), sheung₃ sheung₃ (rising), Sheung₃ hui³ (departing) Sheung₃ yap₄ (entering) the lower series are Ha₃ p'ing₃, ha₃ sheung₃, ha₃ hui,³ and ha₃ yap₄, the middle one being chung¹ yap₄.

Tone marks are given by small figures 1, 2, 3, 4, at the upper right hand corner for higher tones, and the same figures at the lower right hand corner for lower tones; 0 being used for the middle fourth at the end of the word.

Take these sentences in English.

No₁ direct negative, No₁ first low tone.

Did you say no²? no² second high tone (element of surprise).

No₃ surely that cannot be so, No₃ third low tone. There is usually a slight holding on to the sound in this case. It is something like a note of a bell fading away.

You know quite well (strongly affirmative) Know¹ first high tone.

These are not absolute but are frequently used by us in this way.

The method of romanisation is that used in Canton in Romanised Bibles, and a primer of this may be obtained at the Bible store No. 2, Wyndham Street for 15 cts. The primer is not necessary, the sounds are clear, but do not always represent fully the sounds in Cantonese. The English alphabet does not contain certain sounds. Practise your sounds by ear and do not follow the romanised if it conveys the wrong sound to you.

In English we use a sound "er" in speaking.

Chinese use a number of finals such as a, che, ke, kwa, la, le, loh, lok, ma, me, môh, ne, ni, O, wa, and wo.

Some are phonetic, some emphatic, some euphonic, some interrogative, there are about 80 given in Mr. Dyer Ball's "Cantonese made Easy." Language experts may study these, but students will naturally get the usual ones as they learn, a short list is given to assist students, they are not included in the lessons, but some appear in the conversations.

Classifiers or numeratives are common in Chinese. nearly every noun has one, but there are only about 80 in all, a list of 20 is given, others will be learnt in practice. Some come in the lessons, see leesons 2₁; 4₆; 7₁; 8₈; 12₇, etc. They should be learnt by use, the average student cannot learn them all at once and use them correctly. Listen to others and adopt their classifiers. Absolute perfection in this matter is almost impossible in the case of non-Chinese students.

Sounds.— Cantonese sounds are changing, initial l is becoming n; and initial n, l. Variations are found in all districts.

Mistakes.— I fear students may find many mistakes, if they will try this type of proof reading they will see the difficulty.

To err is human, to forgive divine. My humanity may be seen in the errata, let your forgiveness prove your divinity.

Do not be annoyed at the mistakes—correct them and smile.

April 1931.

CANTONESE COLLOQUIAL.

Table of Tone Exercise.

These should be practised frequently at first and occasionally afterwards. When no character is given, no word of the sound given has been found.

	上平 sheung$_3$ p'ing$_1$ first high	上上 sheung$_3$ sheung$_3$ second high	上去 sheung$_3$ hui^3 third high	上入 sheung$_3$ yap$_4$ fourth high	中入 chung$_3$ yap$_4$ middle fourth	下平 ha$_3$ p'ing$_1$ first low	下上 ha$_3$ sheung$_3$ second low	下去 ha$_3$ hui^3 third low	下入 ha$_3$ yap$_4$ fourth low
High / Low	→	↗	↗	⌐	└	—→	↗	↗	⌐
1	因 yan^1	忍 yan^2	印 yan^3	一 yat^4	○	人 yan$_1$	引 yan$_2$	刃 yan$_3$	日 yat$_4$
2	邊 pin^1	貶 pin^2	變 pin^c	必 pit^1	鱉 pit$_0$	○ pin$_1$	○ pin$_2$	便 pin$_3$	別 pit$_4$
3	衣 i^1	椅 i^2	意 i^{c}	○	○	而 i$_1$	耳 i$_2$	二 i$_3$	○
4	央 yeung^1	鞅 yeung^2	怏 yeung^3	○ yeuk^1	約 yeuk$_0$	羊 yeung$_1$	仰 yeung$_2$	樣 yeung$_3$	若 yeuk$_4$
5	謙 him^1	險 him^2	欠 him^3	○ hip^1	怯 hip$_0$	○ him$_1$	○ him$_2$	○ him$_3$	挾 hip$_4$

I am indebted to Mr. Sung Hok P'ang for permission to use this table which was used somewhat in this form by him.

香港・澳門雙城成長經典

6

CONTENTS

英粵通語 Cantonese for everyone —— 香港大學粵語教材（一九三一）

CONTENTS—(*Continued*).

英粵通語 Cantonese for everyone —— 香港大學粵語教材（一九三一）

THE FIRST LESSON

第 一 課—Tai, yat⁴ foh³

1	我	Ngoh₂ (ngaw₂)—*I*	6	有	Yau₂—*Have, is, yes*
2	行	Haang₁—*Walk, go*	7	冇	Mo₂—*Not, no, have not*
3	你	Nei₂ (nay₂)—*You*	8	唔	M₁—*Not, negative*
4	見	Kin° (geen³)—*See, feel*	9	係	Hai₃—*Is, was, to be, Yes*
5	人	Yan₁—*Man, person some one*	10	來, 嚟	Loi₁ lai₁—*To come*

1　我 Ngoh₂

2　我行 Ngoh₂ haang₁

3　你行 Nei₂ haang₁

4　我見你行 Ngoh₂ kin nei₂ haang₁

5　你見人行 Nei₂ kin° yan₁ haang₁

6　有人見我行 Yau₂ yan₁ kin° ngoh₂ haang₁

7　有人行行? Yau₂ yan₁ haang₁ mo₂?

8　我唔見有人行 Ngoh₂ m₁ kin° yau₂ yan₁ haang₁.

9　你係唔係見人行? Nei₂ †hai₃ m₁ hai₃ kin° yan₁ haang₁?

10　有人嚟冇? Yau₂ yan₁ lai₁ mo₂?

1　I.

2　I am walking, or, I walk.

3　You walk

4　I saw you walking.

5　You saw a man walking.

6　There was a man (who) saw me walking.

7　Is there a man walking?

8　I have not seen a man walking.

9　Did you see a man walking?

10　Has a man come?

Two sounds to this word

Another spelling is attached to some words as a guide to those who used my first method, which I think is the easiest method of spelling for English people.

† Hai, m, hai₃. This is a common idiom in Chinese; is, not is? i.e. yes or no?

The First Exercise—(Conversation.)

1 Did you see a man come?
   Nei₂ yau₂ kin³ yan₁ lai₁ mo₂?
   你 有 見 人 嚟 冇?

2 Yes, I saw a man come.
   Yau₂, ngoh₂ kin³ yau₂ yan₁ lai₁.
   有, 我 見 有 人 嚟.

3 Did you see me come?
   Hai₃ kin³ ngoh₂ lai₁ m₁ hai₃?
   係 見 我 嚟 唔 係?

4 No, I saw a person come.
   M₁ hai₂, ngoh₂ kin³ yan₁ lai₁.
   唔 係, 我 見 人 嚟.

5 Did a person see you?
   Yau₂ yan₁ kin' nei₂ mo₂?
   有 人 見 你 冇?

6 Yes, a person saw me.
   Yau₂, yau₂ yan₁ kin³ ngoh₂.
   有, 有 人 見 我.

7 Is anyone walking?
   Yau₂ yan₁ haang₁ mo₂?
   有 人 行 冇?

8 No, no-one is walking.
   Mo₂, mo₂ yan₁ haang₁.
   冇, 冇 人 行.

9 Will you come (or not)?
   Nei₂ lai₁ m₁ lai₁?
   你 嚟 唔 嚟.

10 I will come.
    Ngoh₂ lai₁. 我 嚟.

11 Did you come to see me?
    Nei₂ lai₁ kin³ ngoh₂ hai₃ m₁ hai₃?
    你 嚟 見 我 係 唔 係.

12 Yes, I came to see you.
    Hai₃, ngoh₂ lai₁ kin³ nei₂
    係, 我 嚟 見 你.

THE SECOND LESSON

第 二 課—Tai₃ i₂ foh³

1	个	Koh⁵—*One, a piece, a numerative, or classifier* Koh² *that*
2	兩	Leung₂—*Two, a couple*
3	乜	Mat⁴— *What, who, why*
4	野	Ye₂—*Thing*
5	做	Tso₃—*To make, be, do*
6	佢	K'ui₂—*He, him, she, it*
7	男	Naam₁—*Man, male.*
8	女	Nui₂—*Woman, female, girl*
9	呢	Ni¹ (nee)—*This, (at end of sentence, a question)*
10	啲	Ti¹ (tik⁴) — *This, some, with* ni¹ *and* koh³ *often plural.*

1 有一个人見你行冇? Yau₂ yat⁴ koh³ yan₁ kin³ nei₂ haang₁ mo₂ ?

1 Did a man see you walking ?

2 有，有兩个人見我. Yau₂, yau₂ leung₂ koh⁵ yan₁ kin³ ngoh₂.

2 Yes, two people saw me.

3 乜人嚟. Mat⁴ yan₁ lai₁ ?

3 Who (what man) has come ?

4 你見乜野人嚟. Nei₂ kin⁵ mat⁴ ye₂ yan₁ lai₁?

4 What man did you see coming ?

5 我見人做野. Ngoh₂ kin² yan₁ tso₃ ye₂.

5 I saw a man working (doing something).

6 佢係乜野人呢. K'ui₂ hai₃ mat⁴ ye₂ yan₁ ni¹ ?

6 What kind of person was be ?

7 佢係男人 K'ui₂ hai₂ naam₁ *yan₁.

7 He was a man.

8 係女人唔係呢. Hai₃ nui₂ *yan₁ m₁ hai₃ ni¹ ?

8 Was she a woman?

9 呢个係男人. Ni¹ koh⁵ hai₃ naam₁ *yan₁.

9 This is a man.

10 呢啲係女人. Ni¹ ti¹ hai₃ nui₂ *yan₁.

10 These are women.

†Yare² (without an r sound).

The Second Exercise—(Conversation.)

1   What is that man doing ?

       Koh^2 koh^3 yan_1 tso_3 mat^4 ye_2 ?

       个 个 人 做 乜 野

2   He has come to see you.

       $K'ui_2$ lai_1 kin^3 nei_2.

       佢 嚟 見 你

3   Has this man any work to do ?

       Ni^1 koh^3 yan_1 yau_2 ye_2 tso_3 mo_2 ?

       呢 个 人 有 野 做 冇

4   That man has no work.

       Koh^2 koh^3 yan_1 mo_2 ve_2 tso_3.

       个 个 人 冇 野 做.

5   Has a woman come ?

       Yau_2 nui_2 *yan_1 lai_1 mo_2 ?

       有 女 人 嚟 冇

6   No, no woman has come.

       Mo_2, mo_2 nui_2 yan_1 lai_1.

       冇, 冇 女 人 嚟

7   Has he come to see you ?

       $K'ui_2$ hai_3 lai_1 kin^3 nei_2 m_1 hai_3 ?

       佢 係 嚟 見 你 唔 係.

8   No, he came to see those two men.

       M_1 hai_3, $k'ui_2$ lai_1 kin^5 koh^2 $leung_2$ koh^5 yan_1.

       唔 係, 佢 嚟 見 个 兩 个 人

9   Why did you not come ?

       Tso_3 mat^4 nei_2 m_1 lai_1 ?

       做 乜 你 唔 嚟

10   I had work to do.

       $Ngoh_2$ yau_2 ye_2 tso_3.

       我 有 野 做.

THE THIRD LESSON

第 三 課—Tai₃ saam¹ foh³

1	好	Ho²—*Good, very.*
2	幾	Kei²—*Several, how, fairly.*
3	多	Toh¹—*Many.*
4	要	Iu³—*Want, must, wish*
5	銀	Ngan₁—*Silver, money.*
6	買	Maai₂—*Buy.*
7	少	Shiu°—*Few, small quantity.*
8	得	Tak⁴—*Get, can, able.*
9	去	Hui°—*Go, away.*
10	講	Kong²—*To talk, speak*

---

1 呢啲野好唔好. Ni¹ ti' ye₂ ho² m₁ ho²?

2 个啲幾好. Koh³ ti' kei² ho².

3 幾多个人嚟. Kei² toh¹ koh¹ yan₁ lai₁?

4 你要乜野. Nei₂ iu° mat⁴ ye₂?

5 我要啲銀. Ngoh₂ iu⁸ ti¹ ngan₁.

6 佢買野. K'ui₂ maai₂ ye₂.

7 我有好少銀. Ngoh₂ yau₂ ho² shiu² ngan₁.

8 好多銀買得好少野. Ho² toh¹ ngan₁ maai₂ tak⁴ ho² shiu² ye₂.

9 我要去. Ngoh₂ iu¹ hui³.

10 唔好講人. M₁ ho² kong² yan₁.

---

1 Are these things good or not?

2 Those are very good.

3 How many people are coming?

4 What do you want?

5 I want money.

6 He is buying things.

7 I have very little money.

8 A lot of money will buy very few things

9 I must go.

10 Do not talk about people.

---

* Hui was spelt Hou in the former book. This sound must be carefully practised.

The Third Exercise—(Conversation.)

1 What is this ?

Nı¹ tı¹ hai₃ mat⁴ ye₂ ?

呢 的 係 乜 野

2 That is money.

Koh² ti¹ hai₃ ngan₁.

个 的 係 銀

3 How much money have you ?

Nei₂ yan₂ kei² toh¹ *ngan₁ ?

你 有 幾 多 銀.

4 I have not much money.

Ngoh₃ mo₂ kei² toh¹ ngan₁.

我 冇 幾 多 銀.

5 Is he talking about me ?

K'ui₂ hai₃ kong² ngoh₂ m₁ hai₃ ?

佢 係 講 我 唔 係

6 He is not talking about you, but about going to buy things.

M₁ hai₃ kong² nei₂, kong² hui³ maai₂ ye₂.

唔 係 講 你, 講 去 買 野.

7 Could you arrange not to go ?

Nei₂ m₁ hui³ tak⁴ m₁ tak⁴ ni¹ ?

你 唔 去 得 唔 得 呢

8 I cannot (not go).   I must go.

Ngoh₂ m₁ hui⁸ m₁ tak⁴.

我 唔 去 唔 得

9 Is this good money (silver) ?

Ni¹ koh³ hai₈ ho² *ngan₁ m₁ hai₃ ?

呢 个 係 好 銀 唔 係.

10 That money is not very good.

Koh² koh³ *ngan₁ m₁ hai₃ kei² ho².

个 个 銀 唔 係 幾 好

11 Can I buy things with this money ?

Nı¹ ti¹ *ngan₁ maai₂ tak⁴ ye₂ m₁ ni¹ ?

呢 啲 銀 買 得 野 唔 呢

12 It will buy things, the money is good money.

Maai₂ tak⁴, ti¹ *ngan₁ hai₃ ho² *ngan₁.

買 得, 的 銀 係 好 銀

THE FOURTH LESSON

第 四 課—Tai₂ sz⁵ foh⁵

1	知	Chi²—*Know.*	**6** 聽	T'eng¹—*To hear, listen.*
2	識	Shik⁴—*Know, knowledge.*	**7** 解	Kaai²—*Explain.*
3	咁	*Kom³—So, such.*	**8** 街	Kaai¹—*A street.*
4	樣	*Yeung₃—Style, way, method.*	**9** 條	T'iu₁—*A length, classifier for long things*
5	點	Tim²—*Why, a dot, an hour.*	**10** 路	Lo₃—*A road, a way.*

1 我知你嚟. Ngoh₂ chi¹ nei₂ lai₁.

2 佢唔識你. K'ui₂ m₁ shik⁴ nei₂.

3 呢啲野冇個啲野咁好. Ni¹ ti¹ ye₂ mo₂ koh² ti¹ ye₂ kom³ ho² ?

4 你要幾多樣野呢. Nei₂ iu³ kei² toh¹ yeung₃ ye₂ ni¹ ?

5 點做好呢. Tim² tso₃ ho² ni¹ ?

6 好多人聽佢講. Ho² toh¹ yan₁ t'eng¹ k'ui₂ kong².

7 解我聽得唔得呢. Kaai² ngoh₂ t'eng¹ tak⁴ m₁ tak⁴ ni¹ ?

8 我 去 行街. Ngoh₂ hui³ haang₁ kaai¹.

9 个條係街. Koh² t'iu₁ hai₂ kaai¹.

10 行路去. Haang₁ lo₃ hui³.

1 I knew you were coming.

2 He does not know you.

3 These things are not as good as those.

4 How many kinds of things do you want ?

5 What is the best way to do it ?

6 Many people heard him speak.

7 Can you explain it to me ?

8 I am going for a walk (in the street).

9 That (length) is a street.

10 Walk, or go by road, (on foot).

· Kom is sometimes Kom². Some people use another word but this one will do for both sounds.

Yeung. A large number of words have a changed sound, which often resembles the second high tone or inflection (see yan₁ in lesson 2 No. 7 etc.)

The Fourth Exercise—(Conversation.)

1 Why do you not go ?
    Tim² kaai² nei₂ m₁ hui³ ni¹ ?
    點 解 你 唔 去 呢

2 I do not know the way.
    Ngoh₂ m₁ shik⁴ lo₃.
    我 唔 識 路

3 Do you know how to go to that street ?
    Nei₂ shik⁴ hui³ koh² t'iu₁ kaai¹ m₁ ni¹ ?
    你 識 去 个 條 街 唔 呢

4 You explain to me how to go
    Nei₂ kaai² ngoh₂ t'eng¹ tim² *yeung₃ hui⁵
    你 解 我 聽 點 樣 去

5 This is the way to that street.
    Koh² t'iu₁ kaai¹ hai₃ kom² *yeung₃ hui³.
    个 條 街 係 咁 樣 去

6 Yes, I know.
    Kom² *yeung₃ ngoh₂ chi¹.
    咁 樣 我 知

7 So you know the way, is that so ?
    Kom² nei₂ shik⁴ lo₃, hai₃ m₁ hai₃ ni¹ ?
    咁 你 識 路, 係 唔 係 呢

8 Yes, I know now that you have told me.
    Hai₃, nei₂ kong² ngoh₂ chi¹, ngoh₂ shik⁴ lo₃.
    係, 你 講 我 知, 我 識 路

9 What am I to go to that street for ?
    Hui⁵ koh² t'iu₁ kaai¹ tso₃ mat⁴ ye₂ ni¹ ?
    去 个 條 街 做 乜 野 呢

10 You are to go to buy many things.
    Hui⁵ koh² t'iu₁ kaai¹ maai₂ ho² toh¹ ye₂.
    去 个 條 街 買 好 多 野

THE FIFTH LESSON

第 五 課—Tai₃ ng₂ foh⁵

1	邊	Pin¹— *Which, who, what, side.*		6	茶	Ch'a₁— *Tea.*
2	處	Shue³ (ch'ue⁵)— *Place.*		7	菜	Ts'oi³— *Vegetable, food.*
3	食	Shik₄— *Eat, food.*		8	飲	Yam²— *Drink.*
4	飯	Faan₃— *Rice, food, meal.*		9	完	Uen₁— *Finished, (past tense).*
5	未	Mei₇— *Yet, not yet.*		10	肉	Yuk₄— *Flesh, meat.*

1	佢見邊个人呢. K'ui₂ kin⁷ pin¹ koh⁷ yan₁ ni¹ ?	1	What man did he see ?
2	嚟呢處. Lai₁ m¹ shue³.	2	Come here.
3	我要食的野. Ngoh₂ iu⁵ shik₄ ti¹ ye₂.	3	I want to eat something (food).
4	係食飯唔係. Hai₃ shik₄ faan₃ m₁ hai₇.	4	Is it rice you are eating.
5	你食飯未. Nei₂ shik₄ faan₃ mei₃ ?	5	Have you had (rice) your meal yet ?
6	有啲茶係好. Yau₂ ti¹ ch'a₁ hai₅ ho².	6	Some tea is good.
7	去邊處買菜呢. Hui⁵ pin¹ shue⁵ maai₂ ts'oi³ ni¹?	7	Where do you go to buy vegetables.
8	我食飯, 唔飲茶. Ngoh₂ shik₄ faan₃, m₁ yam² ch'a₁.	8	I will eat rice and not drink tea.
9	佢食完飯未. Kui₂ shik₄ uen₁ faan₃ mei₃ ?	9	Has he finished his meal yet?
10	食肉好唔好呢. Shik₄ yuk₄ ho² m₁ ho² ni¹ ?	10	Is it good to eat meat ?

英粤通語 Cantonese for everyone —— 香港大學粤語教材 （一九三一）

The Fifth Exercise --(Conversation.)

1 Do you know where he has gone ?

Nei₂ chi¹ k'ui³ hui³ pin¹ shue² m₁ chi¹ ni¹ ?

你 知 佢 去 邊 處 唔 知 呢 ?

2 How do I know where he has gone ?

Ngoh₂ tim² chi¹ k'ui₂ hui³ pin¹ shue³ m¹ ?

我 點 知 佢 去 邊 處 呢.

3 I saw him go to that street to buy things.

Ngoh₂ kin¹ k'ui₂ hui³ koh² t'iu₁ kaai¹ maai₂ ye₂.

我 見 佢 去 个 條 街 買 野

4 What did he go to buy ?

Hui¹ maai₂ mat⁴ ye₂

去 買 乜 野

5 He is buying vegetables and meat, a little of each.

Maai₂ ti¹ ts'oi³, maai₂ ti¹ yuk₄, vat⁴ yeung₃ maai₂ ti¹.

買 啲 菜, 買 啲 肉, 一 樣 買 啲

6 Is there nothing much to be bought in that street ?

Koh⁴ t'iu₁ kaai¹ hai₈ m₁ hai₈ mo₂ mat⁴ ye₂ maai₂ ni¹ ?

个 條 街 係 唔 係 冇 乜 野 買 呢

7 No, there are many things to be bought in that street.

M₁ hai₂, koh² t'iu₁ kaai¹ maai₂ tak⁴ ho² toh¹ ye₂

唔 係, 个 條 街 買 得 好 多 野

8 What will you do after your meal ?

Nei₂ shik₄ uen₁ faan₈ tso₈ mat⁴ ye₂ ?

你 食 完 飯 做 乜 野

9 After I have finished my meal (rice) I will go to see two men

Ngoh₂ shik₄ uen₁ faan₂ iu³ hui³ kin³ leung₂ koh² yan₁.

我 食 完 飯 要 去 見 兩 个 人

10 Do not go to see them till they have had their meal (rice).

K'ui₂ mei₃ shik₄ uen₁ faan₃, nei₂ m₁ ho² hui³ kin³ k'ui₂,

佢 未 食 完 飯, 你 唔 好 去 見 佢

香港・澳門雙城成長經典

THE SIXTH LESSON

第 六 課—Tai₃ luk₄ foh³

1	喺	Hai²—*To be in, or at, a place.*	**6**	同	T'ung₁—*With, and, same*
2	時	Shi₁—*Time, an hour*	**7**	鐵	T'it₀—*Iron.*
3	工	Kung¹—*Work.*	**8**	就	Tsau₃—*Then, soon, thus*
4	打	Ta²—*Beat, do.*	**9**	鐘	Chung¹—*Clock, time*
5	錢	*Ts'in₁—*Money, cash*	**10**	想	Seung²—*Desire, wish.*

1 佢喺邊處. K'ui₂ hai² pin¹ shue³ ?

1 Where is he ?

2 我時時食菜. Ngoh₂ shi₁ shi₁ shik₄ ts'oi³.

2 I always eat vegetables.

3 你做乜野工. Nei₂ tso₃ mat⁴ ye₂ kung¹ ?

3 What work do you do ?

4 我做打銀. Ngoh₂ tso₃ ta² *ngan₁.

4 I am a silver smith.

5 幾多个銀錢. Kei² toh¹ koh³ ngan₁ *ts'in₁.

5 How many dollars ?

6 邊个同佢去. Pin¹ koh³ t'ung₁ k'ui₂ hui³ ?

6 Who went with him?

7 呢條鐵唔係幾好. Ni¹ t'iu₁ t'it₀ m₁ hai₃ kei² ho².

7 This piece of iron is not very good.

8 我 就 同 佢 去. Ngoh₂ tsau₃ t'ung₁ k'ui₂ hui³.

8 I will go with him (soon).

9 你幾時去買鐘呢. Nei₂ kei² shi₁ hui³ maai₂ chung¹ ni¹ ?

9 When are you going to buy a clock ?

10 佢想唔嚟. Kui₂ seung² m₁ lai₁.

10 He does not want to come.

The Sixth Exercise—(Conversstion.)

1 Where do you werk ?
Nei₂ hai² pin¹ shue³ tso₋ kung¹ ni¹ ?
你 喺 邊 處 做 工 呢.

2 I work there.
Ngoh₂ hai' koh² shue⁷ tso₃ kung¹.
我 喺 個 處 做 工

3 Do you always work there ?
Nei₂ shi₁ shi₁ hai² koh² shue⁹ tso₋ hai₋ m₁ hai₃ ?
你 時 時 喺 個 處 做 係 唔 係

4 Sometimes (yes) I work there, and sometimes (no) not.
Yau₂ shi₁ hai₋, vau₂ shi₁ m₁ hai₋.
有 時 係, 有 時 唔 係.

5 Can you go with me to buy a clock ?
T'ung₁ ngoh₂ hui⁵ maai₂ yat⁴ koh³ chung¹ tak⁴ m₁ tak⁴ ni¹.
同 我 去 買 一 個 鈍 得 唔 得 呢

6 Where are you going to buy it ?
Hui³ pin¹ shue³ maai₂ ni¹ ?
去 邊 處 買 呢.

7 There are some in that street.
Koh² t'iu₁ kaai¹ yau₂ (lok₀).
個 條 街 有 (咯)

8 When will you come to go with me ?
Nei₂ kei² *shi₁ lai₁ t'ung₁ ngoh₂ hui⁹ ni¹ ?
你 幾 時 嚟 同 我 去 呢.

9 I will come presently (soon).
Ngoh₂ tsau₃ lai₁. 我 就 嚟

10 What price do you want to pay ?
Maai₁ kei² toh¹ *ngan₁ yat⁴ koh³ ni¹ ?
買 幾 多 銀 一 *個 呢

11 Six dollars would be good.
Luk₄ koh³ ngan₁ *ts'in₁ tsau₃ ho².
六 個 銀 錢 就 妤.

12 You cannot buy a good one for as little as six dollars.
Luk₄ koh³ ngan₁ *ts'in₁ kom³ shiu², m₁ maai₂ tak⁴ ho² ye₂.
六 個 銀 錢 咁 少, 唔 買 得 妤 野

個 is the same as 个

THE SEVENTH LESSON

第 七 課—Tai, ts'at⁴ foh°

1	間	Kaan¹—*A classifier for house, a house.* Kaan`—*To partition.*	6	日	Yat₄—*Sun, day.*
2	屋	Uk⁴—*A house, building.*	7	月	Uet₄—*Moon, month.*
3	用	Yung₃—*To use, useful, use.*	8	今	Kam¹—*Now, to-day.*
4	叫	Kiu¹—*To call, to tell.*	9	昨	Tsok₄—*(With day), yesterday, last.*
5	嘅	Ke³—*Sign of possessive, a terminating particle.*	10	番(返)	Faan¹ (faan²)—*Return, come back*

1 呢間係乜野. Ni¹ kaan¹ hai₃ mat⁴ ye₂?

2 个間係屋. Koh² kaan¹ hai₃ uk⁴.

3 你用乜野食飯. Nei₂ yung₃ mat⁴ ye₂ shik₄ faan₃?

4 叫佢嚟. Kiu¹ k'ui₂ lai₁.

5· 啲錢係乜野做嘅. Ti¹ *ts'in₁ hai₃ mat⁴ ye₂ tso₃ ke° ?

6 日日要做好多工. Yat₄ yat₄ iu¹ tso₃ ho² toh¹ kung¹

7 呢个係幾月呢. Ni¹ koh° hai₃ kei² uet₄ ni¹ ?

8 我想今日去佢處. Ngoh₂ seung¹ kam¹ yat₄ hui³ k'ui₂ shue³.

9 昨日冇人嚟. Tsok₄ yat₄ mo₂ yan₃ lai₁.

10 你幾時番嚟？ Nei₂ kei² *shi₁ faan¹ lai₁.

1 What is this (house) kaan ?

2 That is a house.

3 What do you use to eat rice with?

4 Tell him to come.

5 What are the coins made of ?

6 I have a lot of work to do every day.

7 What month is this ?

8 I want to go to his place today.

9 No one came yesterday.

10 When will you come back.

The Seventh Exercise—(Conversation.)

1 Whose houses are these ?
Nı¹ kei² kaan¹ uk⁴ hai₂ pin¹ koh³ ke³ ?
呢 幾 間 屋 係 邊 個 嘅？

2 These houses are mine.
Nı¹ keı² kaan¹ hai₃ ngoh₂ ke³.
呢 幾 間 係 我 嘅.

3 When did you buy them ?
Nei₂ kei⁴ *shi₁ maai₂ ko⁵ ni¹ ?
你 幾 時 買 嘅 呢.

4 I bought them several months ago.
Ngoh₂ maai₂ yau₂ kei² koh° uet₄ (lok₀).
我 買 有 幾 個 月 （略）.

5 You did not ask me to buy for you.
Nei₂ m₁ kiu³ ngoh₂ t'ung₁ nei₂ maai₂.
你 唔 叫 我 同 你 買.

6 Yesterday, I was told that you buy houses.
Tsok₄ yat₄ yau₂ yan₁ wa₃ ngoh₂ chı¹ nei₂ maai₂ uk⁴.
昨 日 有 人 話 我 知，你 買 屋.

7 Did you not know I buy them ?
Nei₂ m₁ chı¹ ngoh₂ maai₂ (*me¹ !) ?
你 唔 知 我 買 （咩!）

8 How could I know ?
Ngoh₂ tim² chı¹ ni¹ ?
我 點 知 呢？

9 I have not seen you for many months.
Ngoh₂ ho² toh¹ koh⁵ uet₄ m₁ kin³ nei₂.
我 好 多 個 月 唔 見 你.

10 I was away elsewhere, and came back to day,
Ngoh₂ hui³ tai₂ i₂ shue³, kam¹ yat₄ faan¹ lai₁.
我 去 第 二 處，今 日 番 嚟.

Me¹ at the end of a sentence is an interrogative sound.

英粵通語 Cantonese for everyone ——香港大學粵語教材（一九三一）

THE EIGHTH LESSON

第 八 課—Tai$_3$ paat$_0$ foh^3

1	話	Wa,—*Speak, say, tell.*	6	使	Shai^2—*To use, need.*
2	大	Taai—*Large, great.*	7	至	Chi^3—*To, to come to.*
3	細	Sai^2—*Small.*	8	陣	Chan$_0$—*A classifier, a short time.*
4	賣	Maai$_3$—*Sell.*	9	前	Ts'in$_1$—*In front, formerly.*
5	都	To^1—*Also.*	10	後	Hau$_3$—*Behind, after*

1 有人話要去買野. Yau$_2$ yan$_1$ wa$_3$ iu$^\circ$ hui$^\circ$ maai$_2$ ye$_2$.

   1 A man says he must go to buy things.

2 佢去大街買野. K'ui$_2$ hui^1 taai$_3$ kaai^1 maai$_2$ ye$_2$.

   2 He went to the big street to buy things.

3 佢買啲好細嘅野. K'ui$_2$ maai$_2$ ti^1 ho^2 sai^3 ke^3 ye$_2$.

   3 He bought some very little things.

4 佢想賣一間屋. K'ui$_2$ seung^2 maai$_3$ yat^4 kaan^1 uk^4.

   4 He wants to sell a house.

5 佢賣做得, 買都做得. K'ui$_2$ maai$_3$ tso$_3$ tak^4, maai$_2$ to^1 tso$_3$ tak^4.

   5 He can sell, and can also buy.

6 佢時時使好多銀. K'ui$_2$ shi$_1$ shi$_1$ shai^2 ho^2 toh^1 *ngan$_1$.

   6 He always uses a great deal of money'

7 佢話要有錢至得. K'ui$_2$ wa$_3$ iu^3 yau$_2$ *ts'in$_1$ chi^3 tak^4.

   7 He said he must have money.

8 佢一陣就去飲茶. K'ui$_2$ yat^4 chan$_0$ tsau$_3$ hui^3 yam^2 ch'a$_1$.

   8 He will go soon (in a moment) to drink tea.

9 我前日去聽人講野. Ngoh$_2$ ts'in$_1$ yat$_4$ hui^3 t'eng^1 yan$_1$ kong^2 ye$_2$.

   9 Two days ago, I went to hear a man talking.

10 後來我同个人行街. Hau$_3$ loi$_1$ ngoh$_2$ t'ung$_1$ koh^3 yan$_1$ haang$_1$ kaai^1.

   10 Afterwards I went with the man for a walk in the street.

The Eighth Exercise—(Conversation.)

1 Did you say some people tell lies ?
Nei₂ wa₃ yau₂ yan₁ kong² taai₃ wa₃, hai₃ m₁ hai ?
你 話 有 人 講 大 話, 係 唔 係?

2 Yes, I said some people tell lies.
Hai₃, ngoh₂ wa₃ yau₂ yan₁ kong² taai₃ wa₃.
係, 我 話 有 人 講 大 話.

3 Have you heard people tell lies ?
Nei₂ yau₂ t'eng¹ yan₁ kong² taai₃ wa₃ mo₂ ni¹ ?
你 有 聽 人 講 大 話 有 呢.

4 Yes, I have heard people tell lies.
Yau₂, ngoh₂ yau₂ t'eng¹ yan₁ kong² taai₃ wa₃.
有, 我 有 聽 人 講 大 話.

5 When did you hear him speak (lies).
Nei₂ kei² *shi₁ t'eng¹ k'ui₂ kong².
你 幾 時 聽 佢 講

6 I hear people talk (lies) every day.
Ngoh₁ yat₄ yat₄ to¹ t'eng¹ yan₁ kong².
我 日 日 都 聽 人 講.

7 Are there so many people who tell lies ?
Yau₂ kom° toh¹ yan₁ kong² taai₃ wa₃, hai₃ m₁ hai₃ ni¹ ?
有 咁 多 人 講 大 話, 係 唔 係 呢.

8 Yes, everyone tells lies, in a moment one may do it.
Hai₃, yan₁ yan₁ yau₂ kong², yat⁴ chan₃ tsau₂ kong²
係, 人 人 有 講, 一 陣 就 講.

9 The day before yesterday I heard some one say so.
Ts'in₁ yat₄ ngoh₂ to¹ t'eng¹ yan₁ kom² kong².
前 日 我 都 聽 人 咁 講.

10 Everyone knows that.
Koh² ti¹ yan₁ yan₁ to¹ chi¹.
个 啲 人 人 都 知.

THE NINTH LESSON

第 九 課—Tai₃ kau² foh³

1	俾 Pei'—*Give, allow.*	6	出 Ch'ut⁴—*Out, go out.*
2	水 Shui²—*Water.*	7	入 Yap₄—*Enter, in.*
3	火 Foh²—*Fire.*	8	牛 Poon³—*Half.*
4	耐 Noi,—*Long time, patience.*	9	年 Nin₁—*Year.*
5	柴 Ch'aai₁—*Wood, firewood.*	10	等 Tang²—*Wait, a class or type.*

1 俾啲茶我飲. Pei² ti¹ ch'a₁ ngoh, yam².

2 飲水好唔好呢. Yam² shui² ho² m, ho² ni¹?

3 飲水係好,飲火水唔好. Yam² shui² hai₃ ho², yam² foh² shui² m, ho².

4 我聽人講好耐. Ngoh₂ t'eng¹ van, kong² ho² noi₃.

5 多人用火柴. Toh¹ yan, yung₃ foh² ch'aai₁.

6 有人出街行冇呢. Yau₂ yan, ch'ut⁴ kaai¹ haang, mo₂ ni¹?

7 有,好多人出出入入. Yau₂, ho² toh¹ yan, ch'ut⁴ ch'ut⁴ yap₄ yap₄.

8 有人打牛日工. Yau₂ yan, ta² poon³ vat₄ kung¹.

9 我做工幾年咁耐. Ngoh₂ tso₃ kung¹ kei² nin, kom³ noi₃.

10 我等上工一年咁耐. Ngoh, tang² sheung₂ kung¹ yat⁴ nin, kom³ noi₃.

1 Give me some tea to drink.

2 Is it good to drink water?

3 Water is good to drink, kerosene is not.

4 I heard people say it long ago.

5 Many people use matches.

6 Have any people gone for a walk (in the street)?

7 Yes, many people are going in and out.

8 Some people work for half the day.

9 I have worked for some years.

10 I have waited for work for a year.

The Ninth Exercise—(Conversation.)

1 Where have you been so long ;
   Nei₂ hui³ pin¹ shue³ kom³ noi₃ ?
   你 去 邊 處 咁 耐

2 I went away to work for a long time.
   Ngoh₂ ch'ut⁴ hui³ ta² kung¹ ho² noi₃.
   我 出 去 打 工 好 耐.

3 How long have you been away ?
   Nei₂ hui˘ yau₂ kei² *noi₃
   你 去 有 幾 耐.

4 I went away for several years.
   Ngoh₂ hui³ kei² nin₁ kom³ noi₃.
   我 去 幾 年 咁 耐.

5 What work did you go to do ?
   Nei₂ hui³ tso₃ mat⁴ ye₂ kung¹ ni¹ ?
   你 去 做 乜 野 工 呢.

6 I went away as a silversmith.
   Ngoh₂ hui ta² *ngan₁.
   我 去 打 銀.

7 Have you been a blacksmith ?
   Yau₂ mo₂ ta² t'it₀ ?
   有 冇 打 鐵

8 No, I cannot do blacksmith's work.
   Mo₂, ngoh₂ m₁ shik⁴ ta² t'it₀.
   冇, 我 唔 識 打 鐵

9 Now you are back, need you go again ?
   Ni¹ chan₃ faan¹ lai₁ m₁ shai² hui⁸ hai₂ m₁ hai₈ ?
   呢 陣 番 嚟 唔 使 去 係 唔 係.

10 I want to go about (in and out), and wait till next year to go.
   Ngoh₂ seung² ch'ut⁴ ch'ut⁴ yap₄ yap₄ tang² ch'ut⁴ *nin₁ chi⁸ hui⁸.
   我 想 出 出 入 入, 等 出 年 至 去

THE TENTH LESSON

第 十 課—Tai₃ shap₄ foh³

1	烟	In¹—*Smoke, tobacco*	6	估	Koo²—*Think, guess*
2	仔	Tsai²—*Boy, small*	7	怕	P'a³—*Fear, think, (afraid)*
3	理	Lei₂—*Manage, control, principle*	8	明	Ming₁, meng₁—*Clear, bright, understand*
4	事	Sz₃—*Affairs, business, matters*	9	白	Paak₄—*White, clear*
5	到	To³—*To come to, arrive*	10	住	Chue₃—*Dwell, live, (present tense, continuous)*

1 你食烟唔食. Nei₂ shik₄ in¹ m₁ shik₄.

    1 Do you smoke (tobacco) or not ?

2 烟仔就食. In¹ tsai² tsau₃ shik₄.

    2 I smoke (eat) cigarettes.

3 唔好理咁多野. M₁ ho² lei₂ kom¹ toh¹ ye₂.

    3 Do not attend to so many things.

4 日日都有好多事做. Yat₄ yat₄ to¹ yau₂ ho² toh¹ sz₃ tso₃.

    4 Every day I have many things to do.

5 佢幾時到呢. K'ui₂ kei² *shi₁ to° ni¹ ?

    5 When did (or will) he arrive ?

6 我估都係呢幾日就到. Ngoh₂ koo² to¹ hai₁ ni¹ kei² yat₄ tsau₃ to°.

    6 I think he will be here during these few days.

7 使乜怕呢? Shai² mat⁴ p'a³ ni¹ ?

    7 Why are you afraid ?

8 明日同你去. Ming₁ yat₄ t'ung₁ nei₂ hui°.

    8 I will go with you to-morrow.

9 明白唔呢. Ming₁ paak₄ m₁ ni¹ ?

    9 Do you understand ?

10 你喺邊處住呢. Nei₂ hai² pin¹ shue³ chue₃ ni¹ ?

    10 Where do you live ?

The Tenth Exercise—(Conversation.)

1 When you were young did you smoke cigarettes ?

Nei₂ sai⁴ koh' koh² shi₁ yau₂ shik₄ in¹ tsai² mo₂ ni¹ ?

你 細 個 個 時 有 食 烟 仔 冇 呢

2 No, when one is young, one cannot smoke.

Mo₂, sai⁵ koh² koh² shi₁ m₁ shik₄ tak⁴ in¹.

冇, 細 個 個 時 唔 食 得 烟

3 Why can he not smoke ?

Tim² kaai² m₁ shik₄ tak⁴ ni¹ ?

點 解 唔 食 得 呢

4 At that time, one is afraid of many things.

Koh² chan₂ shi₁ p'a" ho² toh¹ yeung₃ ve₂ ke⁵.

個 陣 時 怕 好 多 樣 野 嘅

5 What good is smoking ?

Shik₄ in¹ yau₂ mat⁴ ho² ch'ue³ ni¹ ?

食 烟 有 乜 好 處 呢

6 I do not smoke and cannot tell the good of it ?

Ngoh₂ mo₂ shik₄ in¹, wa m₁ ch'ut⁴ yau₂ mat⁴ ho² shue³.

我 冇 食 烟, 話 唔 出 有 乜 好 處

7 Some people smoke when very small (young).

Yau₂ ti¹ yan₂ ho² sai¹ koh³ tsau₂ shik₄ in¹.

有 啲 人 好 細 個 就 食 烟

8 I do not understand why they are allowed to.

Ngoh₂ to¹ m₁ ming₂ paak₄ tim² kaai² pei² k'ui₂ shik₄ ni¹.

我 都 唔 明 白 點 解 俾 佢 食 呢.

9 I (also) cannot attend to so many things.

Ngoh₂ to¹ m₁ lei₂ tak⁴ kom⁵ toh¹ sz₃.

我 都 唔 理 得 咁 多 事.

10 If you want to, you cannot control them.

Seung² lei₂ to¹ lei₂ m₁ to³ ke⁵.

想 理 都 理 唔 到 嘅

11 I do not like listening to so many things.

Ngoh₂ ho² p'a³ t'eng¹ kom² toh¹ ye₂.

我 好 怕 聽 咁 多 野

12 You need not listen unless you like.

Nei₂ m₁ t'eng¹ to¹ tak⁴ ke⁵. 你 唔 聽 都 得 嘅

^ Shue³ is sometimes spoken as ch'ue⁵.

THE ELEVENTH LESSON

第 十 一 課—Tai₃ shap₄ yat⁴ foh³

1	黃	Wong₁—*Yellow, a surname, Mr. Wong.*	6	企	K'ei₂—*To stand, used for residence, home.*
2	色	Shik⁴—*Colour.*	7	門	Moon₁—*Door.*
3	黑	Hak⁴—*Black.*	8	開	Hoi¹—*Open.*
4	攞	Ning¹—*Bring, fetch.*	9	閂	Shaan¹.—*Shut, and fasten.*
5	攞	Loh²—*Get, bring here.*	10	定	Teng₃—*Arrange, determine, fix, or.*

1 呢間係黃屋. Ni¹ kaan¹ hai₃ wong₁ uk⁴.

1 This house is a yellow (coloured) house.

2 要乜野色呢 Iu³ mat⁴ ye₂ shik⁴ ni¹ ?

2 What colour do you want ?

3 黑色都好. Hak⁴ shik⁴ to¹ ho².

3 A dark (colour) will do (be good).

4 攞去我嘅屋. Ning¹ hui³ ngoh₂ ke³ uk⁴.

4 Take it to my house.

5 攞多少銀嚟. Loh² toh¹ shiu² *ngan₁ lai₁.

5 Bring some money (a little), (more or less).

6 做乜你企呢. Tso₃ mat⁴ nei₂ k'ei₂ ni¹ ?

6 Why are you standing ?

7 有人打門. Yau₂ yan₁ ta² moon₁

7 Some one is knocking at the door.

8 等我去開. Tang² ngoh₂ hui³ hoi¹.

8 I will go and open it, (let me, or wait till I open it)

9 閂好門未. Shaan¹ ho² moon₁ mei₃ ?

9 Have you fastened the door yet ?

10 開定唔開. Hoi¹ teng₃ m₁ hoi¹ ?

10 Shall I open it or not ?

The Eleventh Exercise—(Conversation.)

1 Who is knocking (at the door) ?
  Pin¹ koh³ ta² moon₁ ? 邊 个 打 門

2 I knocked.
  Ngoh₂ ta² moon₁ 我 打 門

3 Who are you ?
  Nei₂ hai₃ mat⁴ *yan₁ ? 你 係 乜 人

4 I am Wong₁ Hoi¹ (Hoi¹ is the name, Wong the surname).
  Ngoh₂ hai₃ Wong₁ Hoi¹. 我 係 黃 開

5 Why have you come ?
  Nei₂ lai₁ tso₅ mat⁴ ye₂ ni¹ ? 你 嚟 做 乜 野 呢

6 I came to take some things away (back).
  Ngoh₂ lai₁ ning¹ ti¹ ye₂ faan¹ hui⁵.
  我 嚟 擰 啲 野 返 去.

7 Go in and take them (can).
  Yap₄ hui⁵ loh² tsau₃ tak⁴. 入 去 攞 就 得

8 After taking them, we must fasten the door again.
  Loh² uen₁ ngoh₂ tei₃ iu³ shaan¹ faan¹ moon₁ chi⁵ ho².
  攞 完 我 哋 要 閂 番 門 至 好

9 It is so dark, I do not know how to fasten it
  Kom³ hak⁴ m₁ shik⁴ shaan¹.
  咁 黑 唔 識 閂

10 Tell Ts'in Yung to do it for you (Yung name, Ts'in
  Kiu⁵ Ts'in₁ Yung. t'ung₁ nei₂ shaan¹.   [surname.]
  叫 錢 用 同 你 閂

11 Why is he away so long ? (not come back).
  Kom³ noi₅ k'ui₂ to¹ m₁ faan¹ lai₁
  咁 耐 佢 都 唔 番 嚟

12 He has not fixed any time to be back.
  K'ui₂ m₁ teng₅ kei² shi₁ faan¹ lai₁
  佢 唔 定 幾 時 番 嚟

第 十 二 課—Tai₃ Shap₄ i foh³

1 成	Shing₁—*Complete.*	**6** 頭	T'au₁—*Head, top.*
2 百	Paak₀—*One hundred, all.*	**7** 隻	Cheko — *Classifier for animals, etc.*
3 千	Ts'in¹—*One thousand.*	**8** 手	Shau²—*Hand.*
4 落	Lok₄—*Down, to go down*	**9** 脚	Keuk₀—*Foot.*
5 雨	Ue₂—*Rain.*	**10** 天	T'in¹—*Heaven, sky.*

1 你成日去邊處呢. Nei₂ shing₁ yat₄ hui³ pin¹ shue³ ni¹?

1 Where do you go all day?

2 个處有百幾人. Koh² shue³ yau₂ paak₀ kei² yan₁.

2 There are more than 100 people there.

3 十个百係一千. Shap₄ koh³ paak₀ hai₃ yat⁴ t'sin¹.

3 Ten hundreds make one thousand.

4 我哭落去. Ngoh₂ iu⁵ lok₄ hui³.

4 I must go down.

5 昨日成日落雨. Tsok₄ yat₄ shing₁ yat₄ lok₄ ue₂.

5 Yesterday, it rained all day.

6 有日頭冇. Yau₂ yat₄ *t'au₁ mo₂?

6 Is there any sun (shining).

7 呢隻係乜野呢. Ni¹ chek₀ hai₃ mat⁴ ye₂ ni¹?

7 What is this (chek₀) thing.

8 个隻係手. Koh² chek₀ hai₃ shau².

8 That (chek₀) is a hand.

9 人人有手有脚. Yan₁ yan₁ yau₂ shau² yau₂ keuk₀.

9 Everyone has hands and feet.

10 今日天時幾好 Kam¹ yat₄ t'in¹ shi₂ kei² ho².

10 To-day the weather is (fairly) quite good.

The Twelfth Exercise—(Conversation.)

1 When do you think it will rain ?

Nei₂ koo² kei² *shi₁ yau₂ ue₂ lok₄ ni¹ ?

你 估 幾 時 有 雨 落 呢

2 The weather is so good to day, how can one know when rain will come.

Kam¹ yat₄ t'in¹ shi₁ kom¹³ ho², tim² chi¹ kei² shi₁ yau₂ ue₂ lok₄.

今 日 天 時 咁 好, 點 知 幾 時 有 雨 落

3 Is rain good or not ?

Lok₄ ue₂ ho² m₁ ho¹ ni¹? 落 雨 好 唔 好 呢

4 Sometimes it is good, sometimes it is bad.

Yau₂ shi₁ ho², yau₂ shi₁ m₁ ho².

有 時 好, 有 時 唔 好

5 Well, when is it good ?

Kom² *yeung₃ kei² shi₁ chi⁴ ho² ni¹ ?

咁 樣, 幾 時 至 好 呢

6 When it is needed it is good, when not needed it is bad.

Iu⁵ yung₃ koh² shi₁ tsau₃ ho², m₁ iu³ yung₃ tsau₂ m₁ ho².

要 用 個 時 就 好, 唔 要 用 就 唔 好

7 Can he walk (or not) when it is raining ?

Lok₄ ue₂ koh² shi₁ k'ui₂ haang₁ tak⁴ m₁ haang₁ tak⁴ ni¹ ?

落 雨 个 時 佢 行 得 唔 行 得 呢

8 He can't. He cannot walk when it is raining.

M₁ tak⁴, lok₄ ue₂ koh² shi₁ k'ui₂ m₁ haang₁ tak⁴.

唔 得, 落 雨 个 時 佢 唔 行 得

9 Why cannot he walk ?

Tim² kaai² m₁ haang₁ tak⁴ ni¹ ?

點 解 唔 行 得 呢

10 There is something (wrong) with his foot.

K'ui₂ chek₀ keuk₀ yau₂ sz₃, 佢 隻 脚 有 事

11 Has he asked some one to attend to it ?

Yau₂ kiu³ yan₁ ta² lei₂ mo₂ ? 有 叫 人 打 理 冇

12 Yes, every day he gets a person to attend to it.

Yau₂, yat₄ yat₄ to¹ yau₂ kiu³ yan₁ ta² lei₂.

有, 日 日 都 有 叫 人 打 理

THE THIRTEENTH LESSON

第 十 三 課—Tai₈ shap₄ saam¹ foh⁹

1	面	Min₃ — *Face, surface, the top.*
2	海	Hoi² — *Sea, Ocean.*
3	青	Ts'ing¹ — *Green, blue, clear.*
4	西	Sai¹ — *West.*
5	國	Kwok₀ — *Country, nation.*
6	中	Chung¹ — *Middle, centre.*
7	外	Ngoi₃ — *Outside.*
8	過	Kwoh⁵ — *Pass, over, past, finished.*
9	山	Shaan¹ — *Mountain, hills*
10	睇	T'ai² — *See, observe, look.*

1 你个面有點黑野. Nei₂ koh' min, yau₂ tim² hak⁴ ye₂.

1 Your face has a spot of black on it.

2 有人落海. Yau₂ yan₁ lok₄ hoi².

2 Some people went (down) into the sea.

3 海水係青色. Hoi² shui² hai₃ ts'ing¹ shik⁴.

3 Seawater is a bluish colour.

4 佢係西人. K'ui₂ hai₃ sai¹ yan₁.

4 He is a Westerner, (foreigner).

5 有啲國大, 有啲國細. Yau₂ ti¹ kwok₀ taai₈, yau₂ ti¹ kwok₀ sai³.

5 Some countries are large, and some small.

6 中國有好多人. Chung¹ kwok₀ yau₂ ho² toh¹ yan₁.

6 China has many people.

7 呢啲係外國野. Ni¹ ti¹ hai₃ ngoi₄ kwok₀ ye₂.

7 These are foreign things.

8 今日我要過海. Kam¹ yat₄ ngoh, iu⁵ kwoh⁰ hoi².

8 To-day I must cross the sea (harbour).

9 山邊冇也人行. Shaan¹ pin¹ mo₂ mat⁴ yan₁ haang₁.

9 Not many people walk on the hill side.

10 你睇也野呢. Nei₂ t'ai² mat⁴ ye₂ ni¹ ?

10 What are you looking at ?

The Thirteenth Exercise—(Conversation.)

1 Have you been to foreign countries yet ?

Nei$_2$ yau$_2$ hui^3 kwoh^3 ngoi$_1$ kwok$_0$ mei$_1$ ni^1 ?

你 有 去 過 外 國 未 呢

2 I have been to many countries.

Ngoh$_2$ hui^1 kwoh^3 ho^2 tch^1 kwok$_0$.

我 去 過 好 多 國

3 Do you know foreign languages or not ?

Nei$_2$ shik^4 kong^2 ngoi$_1$ kwok$_0$ *wa$_1$ m$_1$ shik^4 ?

你 識 講 外 國 話 唔 識

4 I can talk a little.

Ngoh$_2$ shik^4 kong^2 toh^1 shiu^2.　我 識 講 多 少

5 What is there to see in foreign countries ?

Hai^2 ngoi$_1$ kwok$_0$ yau$_2$ mat^4 ye$_1$ t'ai^2 ni^1 ?

喺 外 國 有 乜 野 睇 呢

6 There are many things to see in foreign countries.

Hai^2 ngoi$_1$ kwok$_0$ yau$_2$ ho^2 toh^1 ye$_2$ t'ai^2.

喺 外 國 有 好 多 野 睇

7 Are the things there, the same as those here ?

Koh^2 shue^3 ti^1 ye$_2$ t'ung$_1$ ni^1 shue^3 ti^1 ye$_2$ t'ung$_1$ m$_1$ t'ung$_1$ ni^1 ?

个 處 啲 野 同 呢 處 啲 野 同 唔 同 呢

8 Some are like, some are different.

Yau$_2$ ti^1 t'ung$_1$, yau$_2$ ti^1 m$_1$ t'ung$_1$.

有 啲 同 有 啲 唔 同

9 How long were you in foreign lands ?

Nei$_2$ hai^2 ngoi$_1$ kwok$_0$ kei^2 noi$_1$ ni^1 ?

你 喺 外 國 幾 耐 呢

10 I was abroad for several years.

Ngoh$_2$ hai^2 ngoi$_1$ kwok$_0$ kei^2 nin$_1$ kom^3 noi$_1$.

我 喺 外 國 幾 年 咁 耐

11 What do the people there do mostly ?

Koh^2 shue^3 ti^1 yan$_1$ tso$_2$ mat^4 ye$_2$ toh^1 ni^1 ?

个 處 啲 人 做 乜 野 多 呢?

12 There are all kinds, exactly like this place.

Yeung$_1$ *yeung$_1$ to^1 yau$_2$ to^1 hai$_3$ ni^1 shue^3 yat^4 yeung$_3$.

樣 樣 都 有, 都 係 呢 處 一 樣

THE FOURTEENTH LESSON

第 十 四 課—Tai₃ shap₄ sz³ foh⁵

1	先	Sin¹—*Before, formerly.*		6	寫	Se²—*Write.*
2	生	Sha¹ng—*Born, life.*		7	字	Tsz₃ (chi₃)— *Characters, words.*
3	教	Kaau²—*To teach.*		8	曉	Hiu²—*To understand.*
4	讀	Tuk₄—*Read.*		9	樓	*Lau₁—*A floor, storey.*
5	書	Shue¹—*Book.*		10	學	Hok₄—*To learn.*

1 佢頭先嚟. K'ui₂ t'au₁ sin¹ lai₁.

    1 He came a short time ago.

2 佢係黃先生. K'ui₂ hai₃ wong₁ sin¹ shang¹.

    2 He is Mr. Wong.

3 點解你唔 教佢做工呢. Tim² kaai² nei₂ m₁ kaau⁸ k'ui₂ tso₃ kung¹ ni¹ ?

    3 Why do you not teach him to work ?

4 佢讀乜野呢. K'ui₂ tuk₄ mat⁴ ye₂ ni¹ ?

    4 What is he reading ?

5 佢讀書. Kui₂ tuk₄ shue¹.

    5 He is reading a book.

6 我呢幾日要寫好多野. Ngoh₂ ni¹ kei² yat₄ iu³ se² ho² toh¹ ye₂.

    6 These few days, I have to write (many things) a great deal.

7 邊個教你寫字呢. Pin¹ koh³ kaau³ nei₂ se² tsz₃ ni¹ ?

    7 Who teaches you to write ?

8 你曉唔曉呢. Nei₂ hiu² m₁ hiu² ni¹ ?

    8 Do you understand (or not) ?

9 呢間係寫字樓. Ni¹ kaan¹ hai₃ se² tsz₃ *lau₁.

    9 This is the Office.

10 佢學寫字. K'ui₂ hok₄ se² tsz₃.

    10 He is learning to write (characters).

The Fourteenth Exercise—(Conversation.)

1 Can you teach me to read, Sir ?

Sin¹ shang¹, kaau₃ ngoh₂ tuk₄ shue¹ tak⁴ m₁ tak⁴ ni¹?

先 生， 教 我 讀 書 得 唔 得 呢?

2 Yes, what books do you want to read ?

Tak⁴, nei₂ seung² tuk₄ mat⁴ ye₂ shue¹ ni¹ ?

得， 你 想 讀 乜 野 書 呢?

3 I want to learn books for daily use.

Ngoh₂ seung² hok₄ ti¹ yat₄ yung₃ ke³ shue¹.

我 想 學 啲 日 用 嘅 書

4 Have you such books ?

Nei₂ yau₂ kom² ke³ shue¹ mo₂ ?

你 有 咁 嘅 書 冇

5 No, I have no such books.

Mo₂, ngoh₂ mo₂ kom² ke³ shue¹.

冇， 我 冇 咁 嘅 書

6 You must buy them.

Nei₂ iu⁶ maai₂ chi³ tak⁴. 你 要 買 至 得

7 Where can I go to buy them ?

Hui³ pin¹ shue³ maai₂ ni¹ ? 去 邊 處 買 呢

8 They are for sale in the first shop in that street.

Koh² t'iu₁ kaai¹ tai₂ yat⁴ kaan¹ tsau₃ yau₂ tak⁴ maai₃.

个 條 街 第 一 間 就 有 得 賣

9 Are there any in the book store at the University ?

Taai₃ hok₄ shue¹ lau₁ vau₂ mo₂ ni¹ ?

大 學 書 樓 有 冇 呢？

10 I think certainly there are.

Ngoh₂ koo² yat⁴ teng₃ yau₂. 我 估 一 定 有

11 Is that library for the use of students ?

Koh² kaan¹ shue¹ lau₁ hai₃ pei² hok₄ shang¹ yung₃ m₁ hai₃?

个 間 書 樓 係 俾 學 生 用 唔 係

12 Yes, the library is for the students to use

Hai, kaan¹ shue¹ lau₁ hai₂ pei² hok₄ shang¹ yung₃ ke⁶.

係， 間 書 樓 係 俾 學 生 用 嘅

THE FIFTEENTH LESSON

第 十 五 課—Tai₃ shap₁ ng₂ foh³

1	帶	Taai²—*To lead, bring.*		
2	問	Man₃—*To ask.*		
3	洗	Sai²—*To wash.*		
4	房	*Fong₁—*A room.*		
5	身	Shan¹—*The body, one's self.*		
6	熱	It₄—*Hot.*		
7	冷	Laang₂—*Cold.*		
8	晚	Maan₂—*Evening, night.*		
9	起	Hei²—*To arise, get up, begin.*		
10	濕	Shap⁴—*Wet.*		

1 帶佢嚟我處. Taai³ k'ui₂ lai₃ ngoh₂ shue .

    1 Bring him to my place.

2 佢問你有乜野. K'ui₂ man₃ nei₂ yau₂ mat⁴ ye₂ ?

    2 He asks, what have you?

3 俾啲水我洗手. Pei² ti¹ shui² ngoh₂ sai² shau².

    3 Give me some water to wash my hands.

4 呢間房好多人. Ni¹ kaan¹ *fong₁, ho² toh¹ yan₁.

    4 This room has many people (in it).

5 个間係洗身房. Koh² kaan¹ hai₃ sai² shan¹ *fong₁

    5 That room is the bathroom.

6 今日係好熱. Kam¹ yat₄ hai₃ ho² it₄.

    6 To-day is very hot.

7 天冷要熱水洗身. T'in¹ laang₂ iu° it₄ shui² sai² shan¹.

    7 In cold weather we need hot water to wash our bodies.

8 前晚我冇睇書. Ts'in₁ maan₂ ngoh₂ mo₂ t'ai² shue¹.

    8 The night before last I did not read.

9 佢起身未呢. K'ui₂ hei² shan¹ mei₃ ni¹ ?

    9 Has he got up yet ?

10 个條街好濕. Koh² t'iu₁ kaai¹ ho² shap⁴.

    10 That street is very wet.

The Fifteenth Exercise—(Conversation.)

1 Which was hotter, to-day or yesterday ?
Kam¹ yat₄ it₄ teng₃ tsok₄ yat₄ it₄ ni¹ ?
今 日 熱 定 昨 日 熱 呢

2 Both days were equally hot ?
Leung₂ yat₄ to¹ hai₃ kom³ it₄ ?
兩 日 都 係 咁 熱

3 What time do you get up in hot weather ?
T'in₁ it₄ nei₂ kei² toh¹ tim² chung¹ hei² shan¹ ni¹ ?
天 熱 你 幾 多 點 鐘 起 身 呢

4 I get up at six o'clock in hot weather.
T'in¹ it₄ ngoh₂ luk₄ tim² hei² shan¹.
天 熱 我 六 點 起 身

5 What have you to do when you get up ?
Hei² shan¹ yau₂ mat⁴ ye₂ tso₃ ni¹ ?
起 身 有 乜 野 做 呢

6 I wash and have a bath when I get up.
Hei² shan¹ sai² min₃ sai² shan¹.   起身洗面冼身.

7 What floor is the bathroom on ?
Sai² shan¹ *fong₁ hai² kei² *lau₁.   洗身房喺幾樓.

8 The bathroom is on the (second) floor.
Sai₂ shan¹ *fong₁ hai² saam¹ *lau₁.
洗 身 房 喺 三 樓

9 Do you need hot water for a bath ?
Iu⁵ it₄ shui² sai² shan¹ m₁ iu⁵ ni¹ ?
要 熱 水 洗 身 唔 要 呢.

10 No, I do not want hot water for a bath.
M₁ iu³, ngoh₂ m₁ iu³ it₄ shui² sai² shan¹.
唔 要, 我 唔 要 熱 水 洗 身

11 Why is that bathroom so wet ?
Tim² kaai² koh² kaan¹ sai² shan¹ *fong₁ kom⁵ shap⁴ ni¹?
點 解 個 間 洗 身 房 咁 濕 呢

12 I do not know why.
Ngoh₂ to¹ m₁ chi¹ tim² kaai².
我 都 唔 知 點 解

THE SIXTEENTH LESSON

第 十 六 課—Tai₃ shap₄ luk₄ foh³

1	早 Tso²—*Early.*	6	燈 Tang¹—*Lamp.*
2	遲 Ch'i₁—*Late.*	7	快 Faai³—*Quick, happy*
3	夜 Ye₃—*Night, late.*	8	慢 Maan₃—*Slow.*
4	船 Shuen₁—*Ship, boat.*	9	朝 Chiu¹—*Morning.*
5	電 Tin₃—*Electricity, electric.*	10	乾 Kon'—*Dry.*

1 今早我好早起身. Kam¹ tso² ngoh, ho² tso² hei² shan¹

1 This morning I got up very early.

2 點解你咁遲嚟呢. Tim² kaai² nei, kom³ ch'i₁ lai₁ ni¹?

2 Why have you come so late?

3 夜晚有工做. Ye₃ maan, yau, kung¹ tso₃.

3 I have work to do at night.

4 个隻係夜船. Koh²chek₀ hai₃ ye₃ *shuen₁.

4 That is the night boat.

5 電船仔用好多火水. Tin₃ shuen₁ tsai² yung₃ ho² toh¹ foh² shui².

5 Electric launches use a lot of kerosene.

6 呢間屋有電燈. Ni¹ kaan¹ uk⁴ yau, tin₃ tang¹.

6 This house has electric lamps.

7 火船快過電船. Foh² shuen₁ faai³ kwoh³ tin₃ shuen₁.

7 Launches are quicker than electric boats.

8 佢寫字寫得好慢. K'ui, se² tsz₃ se² tak⁴ ho² maan₃.

8 He writes very slowly.

9 今朝我未食野. Kam¹ chiu¹ ngoh₂ mei₃ shik₄ ye₂.

9 I have not eaten anything this morning yet.

10 我要買啲乾電. Ngoh₂ iu³ maai₂ ti¹ kon¹ tin₃.

10 I must buy some dry electricity.

The Sixteenth Exercise—(Conversation.)

1 Where are you going so early ?

Nei₂ kom³ tso² hui³ pin¹ shue³ ni¹ ?

你 咁 早 去 邊 處 呢

2 I am going on board a boat.

Ngoh₂ hui³ lok₄ shuen₁.　我 去 落 船

3 What time does the boat start ?

Chek₀ shuen₁ kei² toh¹ tim² chung¹ hoi¹ shan¹ ni¹ ?

隻 船 幾 多 點 鐘 開 身 呢

4 It starts at 6.30 a.m.

Luk₄ tim² poon³ tsau₃ hoi¹ shan¹.

六 點 半 就 開 身

5 You must go quickly.

Iu³ haang₁ faai³ ti¹ chi³ tak⁴.

要 行 快 啲 至 得

6 I need not be so quick, going slower will not be too late.

M₁ shai² kom³ faai³, maan₃ ti¹ mei₃ ch'i₁.

唔 使 咁 快 慢 啲 未 遲

7 Is the day boat quicker or the night boat ?

Yat₄ *shuen₁ faai³ teng₃ (pe₃) ye₃ *shuen₁ faai³ ni¹?

日 船 快 定 夜 船 快 呢

8 Both are equally quick.

Leung₂ chek₀ to¹ hai₃ yat⁴ yeung₁ faai³.

兩 隻 都 係 一 樣 快

9 Why is it that the nightboat is sometimes so late ?

Tim² kaai² yau₂ shi₁ ye₃ *shuen₁ kom³ ch'i₁ ni¹

點 解 有 時 夜 船 咁 遲 呢

10 If the tide is out it is late.

Shui² kon¹ tsau₃ ch'i₁ ti¹.　水 乾 就 遲 啲

11 Has the steamer electric bells ?

Foh² shuen₁ yau₂ tin₃ chung¹ mo₂.

火 船 有 電 鐘 冇

12 Yes, the steamer has a large electric bell and a small one.

Yau₂ foh² shuen₁ yau₂ taai₃ tin₃ chung¹ yau₂ sai³ tin₃ chung¹.

有, 火 船 有 大 電 鐘, 有 細 電 鐘

香港・澳門雙城成長經典

40

THE SEVENTEENTH LESSON

第 十 七 課—Tai₂ shap₄ ts'at⁴ foh³

1	衫	Shaam¹—*Coat, clothes, dress.*	6	新	San¹—*New.*
2	褲	Foo³—*Trousers.*	7	件	Kin₃—*Classifier for coat, etc.*
3	長	Ch'eung₁—*Long.*	8	淨	Tseng₃—*Clean, only.*
4	短	Tuen²—*Short.*	9	尺	Ch'ek₀—*Foot (measure).*
5	舊	Kau₃—*Old.*	10	寸	Ts'uen¹—*Inch.*

---

1 你啲衫乾未呢． Nei₂ ti¹ shaam¹ kon¹ mei₃ ni¹ ?

1 Are your clothes dry yet ?

2 掟條白褲嚟． Ning¹ t'iu₁ paak₄ foo³ lai₁.

2 Bring a pair of white trousers.

3 佢嘅衫長 *過頭． K'ui₂ ke³ shaam¹ ch'eung₁ *kwoh³ t'au₁.

3 His coat is too long.

4 黃短褲好睇唔好呢． Wong₁ tuen² foo³ ho² t'ai² m₁ ho² ni¹ ?

4 Are yellow short trousers nice to look at ?

5 舊就唔好睇． Kau₃ tsau₃ m₁ ho² t'ai².

5 When old they do not look nice.

6 呢間係新屋． Ni¹ kaan¹ hai₃ san¹ uk⁴.

6 This is a new house.

7 件件衫都係半新舊． Kin₃ kin₃ shaam¹ to¹ hai₃ poon⁵ san¹ kau₃.

7 All the coats are half old (not very new).

8 我件衫洗得好乾淨． Ngoh₂ kin₃ shaam¹ sai² tak⁴ ho² kon¹ tseng₃.

8 My coat has been washed very clean.

9 你有尺冇． Nei₂ yau₃ ch'ek₀ mo₂ ?

9 Have you a foot measure ?

10 我條褲三尺一寸長． Ngoh₂ t'iu₁ foo³ saam¹ ch'ek₃ yat⁴ ts'ue'n ch'eung₁.

10 My trousers are 3 feet and 1 inch long.

The Seventeenth Exercise—(Conversation.)

1 Who washes your clothes for you ?

Pin¹ koh³ t'ung₁ nei₂ sai₂ shaam¹ ni¹ ?

邊 个 同 你 洗 衫 呢

2 I give them to some one to wash.

Ngoh₂ pei² yan₁ sai² ke³.　我 俾 人 洗 嘅

3 Do they wash them clean ?

Sai² tak⁴ kon¹ tseng₃ m₁ ni¹ ?　洗 得 乾 淨 唔 呢

4 Fairly clean.

Kei² kon¹ tseng₃.　幾 乾 淨

5 Are they (newly bought) new ?

Hai₃ san¹ maai₂ ke³ m₁ hai₃ ?

係 新 買 嘅 唔 係

6 No, I bought them long ago.

M₁ hai₃, kau₃ shi₁ maai₂ ke³.

唔 係, 舊 時 買 嘅

7 Are long coats good ?

Ch'eung₁ shaam¹ ho² m₁ ho² ni¹ ?

長 衫 好 唔 好 呢

8 Long coats are good.

Ch'eung₁ shaam¹ ho².　長 衫 好

9 Why are they made so short ?

Tim² kaai² tso₃ kom⁵ tuen² ni¹ ?

點 解 做 咁 短 呢

10 If they are too long they do not look well.

Ch'eung₁ *kwoh³ t'au₁ m₁ ho² t'ai².

長 過 頭 唔 好 睇

11 Are the trousers too long ?

Foo³ keuk₀ ch'eung₁ m₁ ch'eung₁ ni¹ ?

褲 脚 長 唔 長 呢

12 A little too long.

Ch'eung₁ yat⁴ ti¹.　長 一 啲

THE EIGHTEENTH LESSON

第 十 八 課—Tai₃ shap₄ paat₀ foh⁵

1	但	Taan₃—*But, only, however.*	6	方	Fong¹ — *Square, exact, then, place, direction.*
2	擠	Chai¹—*To place.*	7	†地	Tei₃—*Earth, world, land*
3	筆	Pat⁴—*Pen, pencil.*	8	上	Sheung₃—*Above, sheung to go up, ascend.*
4	枝	Chi¹—*Classifier for pens.*	9	*下	Ha₃—*Below.*
5	口	Hau²—*Mouth, classifier for a port.*	10	檯	*T'oi —*A table.*

1 樣樣好, 但呢 樣唔好.
Yeung₃ *yeung₃ho², taan₃ ni¹ yeung₃ m₁ ho².

1 Everything is good, but this kind is not good.

2 你擠乜野喺呢處. Nei₃ chai¹ mat⁴ ye₂ hai² ni¹ shue⁸ ?

2 What did you put here?

3 我後朝早去買筆. Ngoh₂ hau₃ chiu¹ tso² hui³ maai₂ pat⁴.

3 I am going to buy pens, the day after tomorrow in the morning.

4 買幾多枝筆呢. Maai₂ kei² toh¹ chi¹ pat⁴ ni¹.

4 How many pens will you buy ?

5 門口有个人. Moon₁ hau²ʸ yau₂ koh³ yan₁.

5 There is a man at the door.

6 呢樣鐵係四方唔係. Ni¹ yeung₃ t'it₀ hai₂ sz³ fong¹ m₁ hai₃?

6 Is this kind of iron square ?

7 佢間屋有好多地方. K'ui₂ kaan¹ uk⁴ yau₂ ho² toh¹ tei₃ fong¹.

7 There is a lot of space in his house.

8 去買啲上等火柴. Hui³ maai₂ ti¹ sheung₂ tang² foh² *ch'aai₁.

8 Go and buy some of the best matches.

9 樓下有洗身房. Lau₂ ha₃ yau₂ sai⁴ shan¹ fong₁.

9 There is a bathroom downstairs.

10 檯上有一枝電燈. *T'oi₃ sheung₃ yau₂ yat⁴ chi¹ tin₃ tang¹.

10 There is an electric lamp on the table.

† 地 With 口 at side is used for plural of pronouns and men.
ˣ 下 with 口 attached means once, or a short time.

The Eighteenth Exercise—(Conversation.)

1 What do you use to write with ?
Nei, yung, mat⁴ ye₂ se² tsz, ni¹ ?
你 用 乜 野 寫 字 呢

2 I use a pen to write with.
Ngoh₂ yung, pat⁴ se² tsz,. 我 用 筆 寫 字

3 Where will you write ?
Hai² pin¹ shue⁵ se² ni¹ ? 喺 邊 處 寫 呢

4 I will write at the desk.
Hai² se² tsz, *t'oi, se². 喺 寫 字 檯 寫

5 Do you know short hand ?
Nei₂ shik⁴ se² faai⁵ tsz₃ m, shik⁴ ?
你 識 寫 快 字 唔 識

6 I can do type writing, but do not know short hand.
Ngoh₂ shik⁴ ta² tsz₃, taan, hai₂ m, shik⁴ se² faai¹ tsz₃.
我 識 打 字, 但 係 唔 識 寫 快 字

7 Who taught you type writing ?
Pin¹ koh⁵ kaau³ nei₂ ta² tsz₃ ni¹ ?
邊 個 教 你 打 字 呢

8 A westerner taught me type writing.
Yat⁴ koh⁵ sai¹ yan, kaau³ ngoh₂ ta² tsz₃.
一 个 西 人 教 我 打 字

9 How long have you been learning type writing ?
Nei₂ hok₄ ta² tsz, yau₂ kei² *noi₃ ni¹ ?
你 學 打 字 有 幾 耐 呢

10 About two months.
Sheung₃ *ha₃ leung₂ koh³ uet₄. 上 下 兩 个 月

11 Have you to buy typing ribbon ?
Ta² tsz, *taai³ shai² maai₂ m, shai² ?
打 字 帶 使 買 唔 使

12 I need not buy it there is some to use.
M, shai² maai₂ yau₂ tak⁴ yung, a¹.
唔 使 買 有 得 用 吖

THE NINETEENTH LESSON

第 十 九 課—Tai₃ shap₁ kau² foh³

1	木	Muk₄—*Wood.*
2	張	Cheung¹—*A sheet (Classifier).*
3	紙	Chi²—*Paper.*
4	禮	Lai₂—*Propriety, rites, conduct.*
5	拜	Paai³—*Worship, Salute, (with lai₂ — Sunday.)*
6	眞	Chan¹—*True.*
7	熟	Shuk₄ — *Ripe, wellvers-ed, cooked.*
8	牛	Ngau₁—*Cow, cattle.*
9	油	Yau₁—*Oil, paint, butter.*
10	燒	Shiu¹—*Roast, burn.*

1 呢件野係木做嘅. Ni¹ kin₁ ye₂ hai₁ muk₄ tso₁ ke¹.

2 佢有幾張木檯. K'ui₂ yau₂ kei² cheung¹ muk₄ *t'oi₁.

3 你有銀紙冇. Nei₂ yau₂ ngan₁ chi² mo₂.

4 舊時啲人好有禮. Kau shi₁ ti¹ van₁ ho' yau₂ lai₂.

5 今日係禮拜一. Kam¹ yat₄ hai₁ lai₂ paai³ yat⁴.

6 个个女人真係有錢. Koh² koh³ nui₂ *yan₁ chan¹ hai₃ yau₂ *ts'in₁.

7 呢啲肉生定熟呢. Ni¹ ti¹ yuk₄ shang¹ teng₃ (pe₃) shuk₄ ni¹ ?

8 我見一隻大水牛. Ngoh₂ kin¹ yat¹ chek₀ taai₃ shui² ngau₁.

9 你油乜野. Nei₂ yau₁ mat⁴ ye₂?

10 今日有燒牛肉冇？ Kam¹ yat₁ yau₂ shiu¹ ngau₁ yuk₁ mo₂ ?

1 This is made of wood.

2 He has several wooden tables.

3 Have you any bank notes ?

4 People formerly were very polite.

5 To-day is Monday.

6 That woman really has (a lot of) money.

7 Is this meat raw or cooked ?

8 I saw a large water buffalo.

9 What are you painting ?

10 Is there roast beef to-day

The Nineteenth Exercise—(Conversation.)

1 What day (of the week) is it to-day ?
Kam¹ yat₄ hai₃ lai₂ paai³ kei² ni¹ ?
今 日 係 禮 拜 幾 呢

2 To-day is Sunday.
Kam¹ yat₄ hai₃ lai₂ paai³. 今 日 係 禮 拜

3 What is there to eat on Sunday ?
Lai₂ paai³ yau₂ mat⁴ ye₂ shik₄ ?
禮 拜 有 乜 野 食

4 There is plenty to eat.
Yau₂ ho² toh¹ ye₂ shik₄. 有 好 多 野 食

5 I asked you what there was to eat ?
Ngoh₂ man₁ nei₂ yau₂ mat⁴ ye₂ shik₄ ?
我 問 你 有 乜 野 食

6 Look at the table and you will know.
Nei₂ t'ai² *t'oi₁ *min₃ tsau₃ chi¹.
你 睇 檯 面 就 知

7 Are there really so many things ?
Chan¹ hai₃ yau₂ kom³ toh¹ ye₂ *ke³ ?
眞 係 有 吟 多 野 嘅

8 Some people are coming to join us (at the meal).
Yau₂ yan₁ lai₁ shik₄ faan₃. 有 人 嚟 食 飯

9 What do you see on the table ?
Nei₂ kin³ *t'oi₁ *min₃ yau₂ mat⁴ ye₂ ?
你 見 檯 面 有 乜 野

10 I see lettuce and roast beef.
Ngoh₂ kin³ yau₂ shang¹ t'soi³, shiu¹ ngau₁ yuk₄.
我 見 有 生 菜, 燒 牛 肉

11 When are the people coming ?
Koh² ti¹ yan₁ kei² *shi₁ lai₁ ?
个 啲 人 幾 時 嚟

12 They will come directly (soon)
Tang² chan₃ tsau₃ lai₁. 等 陣 就 嚟

THE TWENTIETH LESSON

第 二 十 課—Tai₃ i₃ shap₄ foh³

1	遠 Uen₂—*Far, distant.*	6	窄 Chaak₀—*Narrow.*
2	近 Kan₃(k'an₂)—*Near.*	7	左 Tsoh²—*Left.*
3	車 Ch'e¹—*Carriage, car*	8	右 Yau₃—*Right.*
4	坐 Ts'oh₂—*Sit.*	9	爛 Laan₃—*Broken, damaged.*
5	闊 Foot₀—*Wide.*	10	錯 Ts'oh³—*Error, mistake.*

1 去你處有幾遠呢. Hui³ nei₂ shue³ yau₂ kei² uen₂ ni¹ ?
1 How far is it to your place ?

2 冇幾遠好近. Mo₂ kei² uen₂ ho² k'an₂.
2 Not very far, it is very near.

3 佢有車冇. K'ui₂ yau₂ ch'e¹ mo₂ ?
3 Has he a carriage or not?

4 我出入要坐車. Ngoh₂ ch'ut⁴ yap₄ iu³ ts'oh₂ ch'e¹.
4 When I go about, I must go in a car (carriage).

5 呢間房好闊. Ni¹ kaan¹ *fong₁ ho² foot₀.
5 This room is very large (broad).

6 佢件衫尺寸窄. K'ui₂ kin₃ shaam¹ ch'ek₀ ts'uen⁸ chaak₀.
6 His coat is too narrow (in measurement).

7 个隻係左脚. Koh² chek₀ hai₃ tsoh² keuk₀.
7 That is the left leg.

8 你隻右手好番未呢. Nei₂ chek₀ yau₃ shau² ho² faan₁ mei₃ ni¹ ?
8 Is your right hand well yet ?

9 邊个打爛呢枝燈呢. Pin¹ koh³ ta² laan₃ ni¹ chi¹ tang¹ ni¹ ?
9 Who broke this lamp ?

10 佢講錯. K'ui₂ kong² ts'oh².
10 He spoke wrongly (in error).

The Twentieth Exercise—(Conversation.)

1 Where are you going, that you must walk so quickly ?

Nei, hui³ pin¹ shue³ iu³ haang, tak⁴ kom³ faai³ ni¹ ?

你 去 邊 處 要 行 得 咁 快 呢

2 I have (some) business.

Ngoh, yau₂ sz₃. 我 有 事

3 If you want to be quick, why do you not ride ?

Seung² faai⁵ tim² kaai² m, ts'oh, ch'e¹ ni¹ ?

想 快 點 解 唔 坐 車 呢

4 It costs a lot of money to ride in a car.

Ts'oh₂ ch'e¹ iu³ ho² toh¹ *ngan,.

坐 車 要 好 多 銀

5 How far are you going ?

Nei, hui⁵ kei² uen₂ ni¹ ? 你 去 幾 遠 呢

6 Not very far, it is rather near.

Mo, kei² uen, to¹ kei² k'an,.

無 幾 遠, 都 幾 近

7 I think it is better to ride.

Ngoh, koo² ts'oh, ch'e¹ hui³ ho² ti¹.

我 估 坐 車 去 好 啲

8 Why is it better ?

Tim² kaai² ho² ti¹ ni¹ ? 點 解 好 啲 呢

9 First it is quicker, and second, it does not cost much.

Tai, yat⁴ kin₃ faai³ ti¹, tai₃ i₃ kin₃ m, shai² kei² toh¹ ngan,. 第 一 件 快 啲, 第 二 件 唔 使 幾 多 銀

10 About how much money do you think ?

Nei₂ koo⁵ kei² toh¹ *ngan, kom³ sheung₃ *ha₃ ni¹ ?

你 估 幾 多 銀 咁 上 下 呢

11 I think about $ 1.50

Ngoh, koo² koh³ poon³ *ngan, *ts'in, tsoh² *yau₃.

我 估 個 半 銀 錢 左 右

12 So then it is good.

Kom² to¹ ho². 咁 都 好

48

THE TWENTY FIRST LESSON

第 二 十 一 課—Tai₃ i₃ shap₄ yat⁴ foh³

1	貨	Foh°---Goods	6	美	Mei₂—Beautiful, America
2	貴	Kwai³---Dear, honourable	7	塊	Faai¹—A piece, slice (classifier)
3	計	Kai¹---To reckon, a plan	8	板	Paan²—A board, (of wood)
4	數	Sho°—Figures, numbers, accounts	9	高	Ko¹—High, noble, honourable
5	英	Ying³---Brave, England	10	假	Ka² — False, ka,³ Holiday

1 我想買啲貨. Ngoh₂ seung² maai₂ ti¹ foh³.

1 I want to buy some goods.

2 銀水好高. Ngan₁ shui² ho² ko¹.

2 The exchange is very dear (high).

3 你計乜野呢. Nei₂ kai³ mat⁴ ye₂ ni¹?

3 What are you reckoning?

4 我計數. Ngoh₂ kai³ sho³.

4 I am reckoning accounts.

5 有英國貨到. Yau₂ ying¹ kwok₀ foh¹ to¹.

5 Some English goods have arrived.

6 佢係美國人 K'ui₂ hai₃ mei₂ kwok₀ yan .

6 He is an American.

7 呢塊係乜野. Ni¹ faai³ hai, mat⁴ ye²?

7 What is this piece?

8 个塊係木板. Koh² faai³ hai₂ muk₄ paan³.

8 That is a board (of wood).

9 係唔係好高. Hai₁ m₁ hai₂ ho² ko¹?

9 Is it very high ?

10 唔係, 係假貨. M₁ hai₃, hai₃ ka² foh³.

10 No, it is not the real article.

The Twenty First Exercise—(Conversation)

1 How wide is this board?
Ni¹ faai³ paan² yau₂ kei² foot₀ ni¹ ? 呢塊板有幾闊呢

2 That board is very narrow.
Koh² faai³ paan² ho² chaa₀k. 个塊板好窄.

3 How narrow is it?
Kei' chaak₀ ni¹? 幾窄呢.

4 I reckon it is about 8 inches.
Ngoh₂ kai³ kwoh³ hai₅ paat₀ ts'uen⁵ kom³ sheung₃ *ha₃.
我 計 過 係 八 寸 咁 上 下

5 Is it really so narrow?
Chan¹ hai₃ kom³ chaak₀? 真 係 咁 窄

6 Do you think it is false, I do not tell lies.
Nei₂ koo² ka² ke³, ngoh₂ mo₂ kong² taai₃ wa₃ ke³.
你 估 假 嘅, 我 冇 講 大 話 嘅

7 So narrow, how much meney do you want for it ?
Kom³ chaak₀, iu⁵ kei² toh¹ *ngan₁ ni¹?
咁 窄, 要 幾 多 銀 呢.

8 Why is it so dear?
Tim² kaai² tak⁴ kom³ kwai³ ni¹?
點 解 得 咁 貴 呢.

9 You say it is very dear.
Nei₂ wa₃ ho² kwai³. 你 話 好 貴

10 Exchange (silver) is very high.
Ngan₁ shui² ho² ko¹. 銀 水 好 高.

11 Are the goods American or English?
Hai₃ mei₂ kwok₀ foh³ ting₃ (pe.) ying¹ kwok₀ foh³ ni¹ ?
係 美 國 貨 定 英 國 貨 呢

12 They are American.
Hai₅ mei₁ kwok₀ foh³. 係 美 國 貨.

' Often a sound like er is used in place of Ting₃

THE TWENTY SECOND LESSON

第 二 十 二 課—Tai₂ i₃ shap₁ i₃ foh³

1	倉	Ts'ong¹—*A godown, hold.*	6	銅	T'ung₁—*Brass, copper.*
2	深	Sham¹—*Deep.*	7	分	Fan¹—*Divide, distinguish.* Fan³—*A share or portion.*
3	淺	Ts'in²—*Shallow.*	8	重	Ch'ung₃—*Heavy,* chung₃ *besides, important.*
4	內	Noi₃—*Inside.*	9	實	Shat₄—*Solid, true, firm.*
5	物	Mat₄—*Articles, matter, material.*	10	心	Sam¹—*Heart, mind.*

1 呢間係貨倉. Ni¹ kaan¹ hai₃ foh³ ts'ong¹.

2 貨倉有幾深呢. Foh⁵ ts'ong¹ yau₂ kei²sham¹ni¹?

3 冇幾深, 好淺. Mo₂ kei² sham¹, ho² ts'in².

4 倉內有乜野貨呢. Ts'ong¹ noi₃ yau₂ mat⁴ ye₂ foh³ ni¹?

5 有啲火水, 樣樣物件都有. Yau₂ ti¹ foh² shui², yeung₃*yeung₃mat₄*kin₃ to¹ yau₂.

6 有銅冇呢? Yau₂ t'ung₁ mo₂ ni¹?

7 係分開擠唔係呢? Hai₃ fan¹ hoi¹ chai¹ m₁ hai₃ ni¹?

8 銅重定鐵重呢? T'ung₁ ch'ung₂ ting₃ (pe₃) t'it₀ ch'ung₂ ni¹?

9 唔話得實. M₁ wa₃ tak⁴ shat₁.

10 有啲係實心嘅. Yau₂ ti¹ hai₃ shat₄ sam¹ ke³.

1 This is a godown.

2 What is the depth of this godown?

3 Not very deep, it is very shallow.

4 What goods are in this godown?

5 There is some kerosene, and all kinds of things.

6 Is there any copper?

7 Are they stored separately?

8 Is copper heavier or iron?

9 I cannot say certainly (for certain).

10 Some of it is solid.

The Twenty Second Exercise—(Conversation.)

1 Have you ordered goods ?

Nei₂ yau₂ †teng, foh³ mo₂ ? 你 有 定 貨 冇

2 The last few months I have not ordered any.

Ni¹ kei² koh³ uet₄ ngoh₂ mo, teng₅ foh° 呢 幾 个 月 我 冇 定 貨

3 Why do you not order ?

Tim² kaai² m₁ teng₅ ni¹ ? 點 解 唔 定 呢

4 I see that every thing is in a bad way.

Ngoh₂ kin° yeung, yeung₂ to¹ m, hai, ho². 我 見 樣 樣 都 唔 係 好

5 How much goods have you in the godown ?

Foh³ ts'ong¹ yau₂ kei² toh¹ foh³ ni¹ ? 貨 倉 有 幾 多 貨 呢

6 I still have a large quantity.

Chung, yau₂ l o² toh¹. 重 有 好 多

7 Do you want to order at once or not ?

Shai² t om' faai³ teng, m₁ shai² ? 使 咁 快 定 唔 使

8 I need not order so soon.

M₁ shai² teng, kom' faai³. 唔 使 定 咁 快

9 Copper and iron are not dear.

T'ung₁ t'it₀ m₁ hai₅ kwai°. 銅 鐵 唔 係 貴

10 I know they are not dear, but I have no money to buy them.

Ngoh₂ chi¹ m₁ hai, kwai°, taan₅ ngoh₂ mo₂ *ts'in₁ maai₂. 我 知 唔 係 貴, 但 我 冇 錢 買

11 If you have no money, you can pay in instalments.

Nei₂ mo₂ *ts'in,₁ fan¹ hoi¹ pei² to¹ tak⁴. 你 冇 錢 分 開 俾 都 得

12 I must consider the matter even if I may pay in instalments

Fan¹ hoi¹ pei² ngoh, to¹ iu³ seung² kwoh³ chi° tak⁴ 分 開 俾 我 都 要 想 過 至 得

† Teng   A longer sound.

THE TWENTY THIRD LESSON

第 二 十 三 課—Tai i, chap, saam¹ foh³

1	便	P'in₃—Convenient, side	6	補	Po²—To repair.
2	紅	Hung₁—Red.	7	爐	Lo₁—A boiler.
3	藍	Laam₁—Blue.	8	聞	Man₁—To hear.
4	旗	K'ei₁—A flag.	9	掃	So³—To sweep, a broom.
5	椅	I'—A chair.	10	釘	Teng¹—A nail.

1 我左手便屋有个西人.
Ngoh₂ tsoh² shau² pin₃ uk⁴ yau₂ koh¹ sai¹ yan .
— There is a westerner in the house at my left.

2 佢嘅面係紅色. K'ui₂ ke³ min₃ hai₃ hung₁ shik⁴
— His face is red.

3 呢張紙係藍色. Ni¹ cheung¹ chi² hai₃ laam₁ shik⁴.
— This paper is blue.

4 呢枝係半白半紅旗. Ni¹ chi¹ hai₃ poon³ paak₄ poon³ hung₁ k'ei₁.
— This flag is half white and half red.

5 个張係四方椅. Koh³ cheung¹ hai₃ sz¹ fong¹ i².
— That is a square chair.

6 佢補衫. K'ui₂ po³ shaam¹
— He repairs clothes (coats)

7 我做補爐. Ngoh₂ tso po² lo₁.
— I repair boilers.

8 你聞得人講係唔係. Nei₂ man₁ tak⁴ yan₁ kong² hai₃ m₁ hai₃ ?
— Did you hear some one say it?

9 快啲掃乾淨啲地方. Faai³ ti¹ so³ kon¹ tseng₃ ti¹ tei₂ fong .
— Quickly sweep the place clean.

10 俾一口釘我. Pei³ yat⁴ hau² teng¹ ngoh₂.
— Give me a nail

The Twenty Third Exercise—(Conversation.)

1 What is the weather like to day?

Kam¹ yat₄ t'in¹ shi₁ tim² *yeung₆ ni¹?

今 日 天 時 點 樣 呢

2 It is very cold to day.

Kam¹ yat₄ ho² laang₂. 今 日 好 冷

3 What can we do as it is cold?

Kom³ laang₂ ngoh₂ iu³ tim² *yeung₃ ni¹?

咁 冷 我 要 點 樣 呢

4 As we have a stove we need not fear.

Yau₂ foh² lo₁ m₁ p'a³. 有 火 爐 唔 怕

5 You must (sweep) clean your stove.

Nei₂ koh³ foh² lo₁ iu³ so⁵ kwoh³ chi³ ta√.

你 個 火 爐 要 掃 過 至 得

6 I will call a servant to clean it soon.

Ngoh₂ yat⁴ *chan₃ tsau₃ kiu³ koh³ kung¹ yan₁ so³.

我 一 陣 就 叫 ·個 工 人 掃

7 What is that on the mantelpiece?

Foh² lo₁ t'au₁ koh² ti¹ hai₃ mat⁴ ye₂?

火 爐 頭 個 啲 係 乜 野

8 Those things on the mantelpiece are newspapers.

Foh² lo₁ t'au₁ koh² kei² cheung¹ hai₃ san¹ man₁ chi².

火 爐 頭 個 幾 張 係 新 聞 紙

9 Bring a chair for me.

Ning¹ cheung¹ i² lai₁ ngoh₂. 擰 張 椅 嚟 我

10 What do you want a chair for?

Nei₂ iu³ i² lai₁ tso₃ mat⁴ ye₂?

你 要 椅 嚟 做 乜 野

11 I want a chair to sit on, and see (read) the newspapers?

Ngoh₂ iu⁵ i¹ lai₁ ts'oh₄ hai² shue⁵ t'ai² san¹ man₁ chi².

我 要 椅 嚟 坐 喺 處 睇 新 聞 紙

12 There was a lot of news in yesterday's paper.

Tsok₄ yat₄ san¹ man₁ chi² yan₂ ho⁴ toh¹ ye₂ maai₈.

昨 日 新 聞 紙 有 好 多 野 賣

THE TWENTY FOURTH LESSON

第 二 十 四 課—Tai₃ i₃ shap₄ sz³ foh³

1	變	Pin³—Change.	6 老	Lo₂—Old, aged.
2	凍	Tung⁵—Cold.	7 請	Ts'ing²—Request, invite.
3	暖	Nuen₂—Warm.	8 東	Tung¹—East.
4	布	Po³—Cloth, spread out.	9 南	Naam₁—South.
5	搵	Wen²—Seek, find.	10 北	Pak⁴—North.

1 你件衫變色 Nei₂ kin₂ shaam¹ pin³ shik⁴

1 Your coat has changed in colour.

2 凍水洗身好凍 Tung³ shui² sai² shan¹ ho² tung³.

2 It is very cold to wash in cold water.

3 今日暖番啲 Kam¹ yat₄ nuen₂ faan¹ ti¹.

3 It is warmer again to-day.

4 我要買啲布嚟做衫 Ngoh₂ iu³ maai₂ ti¹ po³ lai₁ tso shaam¹.

4 I must buy some cloth to make a coat.

5 有人搵你 Yau₂ yan₁ wan² nei₂.

5 Some one is looking for you.

6 佢有幾老呢 K'ui₂ yau₂ kei² lo₂ ni¹?

6 How old is he?

7 昨日有人請我飲茶 Tsok₄ yat₄ yau₂ yan₁ ts'ing² ngoh₂ yam² ch'a₁.

7 Yesterday a person invited me to (drink) tea.

8 遠東有好多國 Uen₂ tung¹ yau₂ ho² toh¹ kwok₀

8 In the Far East there are many countries.

9 南方都幾熱 Naam₁ fong¹ to¹ kei² it₁.

9 The south is fairly hot.

10 你去過英國北便未呢 Nei₂ hui⁵ kwoh³ ying¹ kwok₀ pak⁴*pin₃ mei₃ ni¹?

10 Have you been to the North of England yet?

The Twenty Fourth Exercise—(Conversation.)

1 The weather is always changing.
T'in¹ shik⁴ shi₁ shi₁ pin³. 天 色 時 時 變

2 Yes, it is uncertain.
Hai-, mo₂ teng₃ ke³. 係, 冇 定 嘅.

3 The South and North are different.
Naam₁ fong¹ Pak⁴ fong¹ hai₃ m₁ t'ung₁.
南 方 北 方 係 唔 同.

4 How are they different?
Yau₂ mat⁴ m₁ t'ung₁ ni¹? 有 乜 唔 同 呢.

5 They are different in temperature, (hot and cold)
Yat⁴ laang₂ yat⁴ it₄ tsau₁ m₁ t'ung₁.
一 冷 一 熱 就 唔 同

6 I fear the cold very much.
Ngoh₂ ho² p'a³ laang₂ ke³. 我 好 怕 冷 嘅

7 How can you fear as you have so money clothes?
Nei₂ yau₂ kom³ toh¹ shaam¹, p'a³ mat⁴ ye₂ ni¹?
你 有 咁 多 衫 怕 乜 野 呢.

8 Having so many clothes is not convenient.
Yau₂ shaam¹ to¹ m₁ fong¹ pin, ke¹.
有 衫 都 唔 方 便 嘅.

9 How is it inconvenient ?
Yau₂ mat⁴ ye₂ m₁ fong¹ pin₁ ni ?
有 乜 野 唔 方 便 呢.

10 To speak of nothing else, it is not convenient for going about (in and out).
Ch'ut⁴ yap₄ tsau₁ m₁ fong¹ pin₁, m₁ shai³ kong² tai₁
i₃ *yeung₃. 出 入 就 唔 方 便,唔 使 講 第 二 樣

11 It is better to live in the tropics.
Chue₃ it₄ taai³ tei₃ fong¹ ho² ti¹ ke³.
住 熱 帶 地 方 好 的 嘅.

12 That is certainly so.
Yat⁴ ting₁ hai₃. 一 定 係.

THE TWENTY-FIFTH LESSON

第 二 十 五 課—Tai₃ i₃ shap₄ ng₂ foh³

1	盤	P'oon₁—A dish, a classifier, examine.
2	算	Suen³—Reckon, regard, estimate.
3	部	Po₃—Classifier for book, a department.
4	唐	T'ong₁—Chinese, name of dynasty.
5	作	Tsok₀ — Make, do, be, regard as.
6	文	Man₁—Literature, composition, literary style
7	章	Cheung¹ — A chapter, (man₁ cheung¹) essay.
8	程	Ch'ing₁—A route, (cheung¹ ch'ing₁), scheme, regulation.
9	墨	Mak₄—Ink.
10	嘓	Choh³ (Jaw²) — Finish, past tense.

1 呢个面盤幾好. Ni¹ koh³ min₃ *p'oon₁ kei² ho².
1 This wash basin is rather good.

2 我想學算數. Ngoh₂ seung² hok₄ suen³ sho³.
2 I want to learn arithmetic.

3 我買三部書嚟學. Ngoh₂ maai₂ saam¹ po₃ shue¹ lai₁ hok₄.
3 I am buying three books to learn (from).

4 係買唐書唔係呢. Hai₃ maai₂ t'ong₁ shue¹ m₁ hai₃ ni¹?
4 Are you buying Chinese books?

5 好多人作書教人. Ho² toh¹ yan₁ tsok₀ shue¹ kaau³ yan₁.
5 Many people make books to teach.

6 我買書嚟學作文. Ngoh₂ maai₂ shue¹ lai₁ hok₄ tsok₀ man₁.
6 I am buying books to learn to write composition.

7 呢章係乜野書呢. Ni¹ cheung¹ hai₃ mat₄ ye₂ shue¹ ni¹?
7 What is this chapter?

8 个章係教人學唐話嘅章程. Koh² cheung¹ hai₃ kaau³ yan₁ hok₄ t'ong₁ *wa₃ ke³ cheung¹ ch'ing₁.
8 That chapter is a method for teaching people to speak Chinese.

9 你有買墨水筆有? Nei₂ yau₂ maai₂ mak₄ shui² pat⁴ mo₂?
9 Have you bought a pen?

10 有, 墨水筆咁有用, 我買嘓好耐. Yau₂, mak₄ shui² pat⁴ kom³ yau₂ yung₃, ngoh₂ maai₂ choh² ho² noi₃ (lo³).
10 Yes, a pen is so useful, and I bought one a long time ago.

The Twenty-fifth Exercise—(Conversation.)

1 Sir, please teach me to read.

Sin¹ shaang¹ ts'ing² nei₂ kaau³ ngoh₂ tuk₄ shue¹.

先 生 請 你 教 我 讀 書

2 What books do you want to read?

Nei₂ seung² tuk₄ mat¹ ye₂ shue¹?

你 想 讀 乜 野 書

3 I want to read Chinese books and write Chinese characters

Ngoh₂ seung² tuk₄ t'ong₁ shue¹ se² t'ong₁ tsz₃.

我 想 讀 唐 書 寫 唐 字

4 Have you bought books yet?

Yau₂ maai₂ to² shue¹ mei₂ ni¹? 有 買 倒 書 未 呢

5 Please buy three books for me.

Ts'ing² sin¹ shaang¹ t'ung₁ ngoh₂ maai₂ saam¹ po₃.

請 先 生 同 我 買 三 部

6 In writing Chinese words one must learn Chinese Composition.

Se² t'ong₁ tsz₃ iu³ hok₄ tsok₀ t'ong₁ man₁.

寫 唐 字 要 學 作 唐 文

7 Some say one must learn to write essays.

Yau₂ yan₁ wa₂ iu³ hok₄ tsok₀ man₁ cheung¹.

有 人 話 要 學 作 文 章

8 One must work hard to learn essay writing.

Seung² hok₄ tsok₀ man₁ cheung¹ iu³ ho² yung₂ sam¹ chi³ tak⁴

想 學 作 文 章 要 好 用 心 至 得

9 Have you learnt arithmetic yet?

Nei₂ hok₄ suen³ sho³ mei₃ ni¹? 你 學 算 數 未 呢

10 I want to buy an abacus to learn.

Ngoh₂ seung² maai₂ suen³ p'oon₁ lai₁ hok₄.

我 想 買 算 盤 嚟 學

11 You can use pen and ink to reckon with.

Yung₃ pat⁴ mak₄ kai³ sho² to¹ tak⁴ (lo³).

用 筆 墨 計 數 都 得

THE TWENTY SIXTH LESSON

第 二 十 六 課—Tai, i₃ shap₄ luk₄ foh.

1	親	Ts'an¹— *Near, relations, self.*	6	姊	Tsz²—*Elder sister.*
2	父	Foo,—*Father.*	7	妹	Mooi,—*Younger sister.*
3	母	Mo₂—*Mother.*	8	友	Yau,—*Friend.*
4	兄	Hing¹—*Elder brother.*	9	朋	P'ang,—*Friend, (used with yau)*
5	弟	Tai,—*Younger brother.*	10	佬	Lo⁷—*A person, fellow*

1 我親身去見佢 Ngoh₂ ts'an¹ shan¹ hui³ kin³ k'ui₂.

1 I went myself (in person) to see him.

2 我父親喺屋†企做工 Ngoh₂ foo, ts'an¹ hai² uk⁴ k'ei² tso, kung¹.

2 My father is at home working.

3 佢母親就嚟見佢 K'ui₂ mo₂ ts'an¹ tsau, lai, kin° k'ui₂.

3 His mother is coming soon to see him.

4 家兄唔喺屋企 Ka¹ hing¹ m₁ hai² uk⁴ k'ei².

4 (My) elder brother is not at home.

5 我有四兄弟，一个大，兩个細同我係四兄弟 Ngoh₂ yau₂ sz³ hing¹ tai,, yat⁴ koh³ taai₃, leung₂ koh³ sai° t'ung₁ ngoh₂ hai₃ sz³ hing¹ tai,.

5 I have four brothers, one elder brother, two younger brothers and myself, being four brothers.

6 你大姊去邊處呢 Nei₂ taai, tsz² hui⁸ pin¹ shue³ ni¹?

6 Where has your elder sister gone?

7 佢同我个妹去上海. K'ui, t'ung₁ ngoh₂ koh³ *mooi₃ hui³ sheung₈ hoi².

7 She has gone to Shanghai with my younger-sister.

8 我有好多書友 Ngoh₂ yau₂ ho² toh¹ shue¹ *yau₂.

8 I have many school fellows.

9 佢有三个朋友 K'ui₂ yau₂ saam¹ koh⁹ p'ang₁ yau₂.

9 He has three friends.

10 打鐵工人叫做打鐵佬 Ta² t'it₀ kung¹ yan₁ kiu⁸ tso₃ ta² t'it₀ lo².

10 Workers in iron, are called iron worker fellows

†Note 跥 K'ei² is more frequently used for family or home.

The Twenty Sixth Exercise—(Conversation.)

1 Sir, I wish to go home for a few days.

Sin¹ shaang¹, ngoh₂ seung² faan¹ uk⁴ ke'i² kei² yat₄

先生，我想番屋企幾日

2 Why do you want to go home?

Tso₃ mat⁴ iu⁵ faan¹ uk⁴ k'ei² ni¹?

做乜婓番屋企呢

3 My parents tell me to go.

Ngoh₂ foo₃ mo₂ kiu₁ ngoh₂ hui⁵

我父母叫我去

4 What is the matter?

Yau₂ mat⁴ ye₂ sz₃ ni¹? 有乜野事呢.

5 My mother has some business.

Ngoh₂ mo₂ ts'an¹ yau₂ ti¹ sz₃ 我母親有啲事.

6 Is it your brothers' affairs?

Hai₃ m₁ hai₃ nei₂ hing¹ tai₃ ke⁵ sz₃ ni¹?

係唔係你兄弟嘅事呢

7 I do not know.   My mother is not very well.

Ngoh₂ m₁ chi¹ a¹,   ngoh₂ lo₂ *mo₂ m₁ hai₃ kei² ho².

我唔知吖，我老母唔係幾好

8 Why do your sisters not attend to her?

Tso₃ mat⁴ nei₂ tsz² *mooi₃ m₁ pei² ye₂ k'ui₂ shik₄ ni¹?

做乜你姊妹唔俾野佢食呢.

9 My sisters are young.

Ngoh₂ tsz² *mooi₃ sai³ koh³. 我姊妹細个.

10 Why must (want) you go?

Tim² kaai² iu⁵ nei₂ hui⁵ ni¹? 點解要你去呢.

11 My mother has a cold and fever.

Ngoh₂ lo₂ *mo₂ laang₂ ts'an¹, shan¹ it₄ 我老母冷親身熱.

12 Well, you must come back quickly.

Ho² a³, nei₂ iu⁵ faai⁵ ti¹ faan¹ lai₁

好呀，你要快啲番嚟

THE TWENTY-SEVENTH LESSON

第 二 十 七 課—Tai₃ i₃ shap₄ ts'at⁴ foh³

1	每	Mooi₂—*Each, every.*	**6**	即	Tsik⁴—*At once, immediately.*
2	歲	Sui³—*Year, (of age).*	**7**	刻	Hak⁴—*Cut, carve, moment.*
3	添	T'im¹—*Increase, further, add.*	**8**	晏	Aan³—*Late, noon.*
4	晨	Shan₁—*Period, morning.*	**9**	期	K'ei₁—*Date, fixed time.*
5	初	Ch'oh¹—*Beginning, first.*	**10**	滿	Moon₂—*Full.*

1 你每日幾點鐘起身呢. Nei₂ mooi₂ yat₄ kei² tim² chung¹ hei² shan¹ ni¹ ?

1 What time do you get up every day ?

2 年年起頭，人人加一歲. Nin₁ Nin₁ hei²*t'au₁, yan₁ yan₁ ka¹ yat⁴ sui³.

2 At the beginning of each year, every one adds one year to his age.

3 你咁講就添一歲. Nei₂ kom⁴ kong² tsau₃ t'im¹ yat⁴ sui³.

3 When you say that, you mean that they add a year to their age.

4 朝早見人，就話早晨. Chiu¹ tso² kin³ yan₁, tsau₃ wa₃ tso² shan₁.

4 When you see people early, you say " Good morning " (early time).

5 初初起身你做乜野呢. Ch'oh¹ ch'oh¹ hei² shan¹ nei₂ tso₃ mat⁴ ye₂ ni¹ ?

5 When you first get up what do you do?

6 初初起身係即時讀書唔係. Ch'oh¹ ch'oh¹ hei² shan¹ hai₃ tsik⁴ shi₁ tuk₄ shue¹ m₁ hai₃.

6 When you get up do you read immediately ?

7 唔係即刻讀書，係洗面先. M₁ hai₃ tsik⁴ hak⁴ tuk₄ shue¹, hai₃ sai² min₃ sin¹.

7 No, I do not read at once, I wash my face first.

8 你讀書讀到好晏. Nei₂ tuk₄ shue¹ tuk₄ to⁴ ho² aan³.

8 Do you read till late in the morning ?

9 一年有幾多个學期呢. Yat⁴ nin₁ yau₂ kei² toh¹ koh³ hok₄ k'ei₁ ni¹ ?

9 How many terms are there in the (school).

10 有三个學期，呢个學期就滿. Yau₂ saam¹ koh³ hok₄ k'ei₁, ni¹ koh³ hok₄ k'ei₁ tsau₃ moon₂.

10 There are three terms. This term is nearly ended (full).

The Twenty-seventh Exercise—(Conversation.)

1 Good morning, have you had your breakfast (rice) yet ?

Tso² shan₁, shik₄ faan₃ mei₃ ni¹?　早晨,食飯未呢.

2 Not yet, have you eaten yet ?

Mei₃ a¹, nei₂ shik₄ choh² mei₃ ni¹?
未吖, 你 食 咗 未 呢 .

3 I have eaten. What time do you breakfast every morning ?

Shik₄ choh² lok₀, nei₂ mooi₂ chiu¹ kei² tim² chung¹
shik₄ faan₃ ni¹?　食咗咯,你每朝幾點鐘食飯呢.

4 We eat very late (in the morning)?

Ngoh₂ tei₃ ho² aan³ shik₄ faan₃ ke′.
我 地 好 晏 食 飯 嘅 .

5 Why you are so late ?

Tim² kaai² kom³ aan³ ni¹?　點解咁晏呢.

6 We are always so.

Ngoh₂ tei₃ shi₁ shi₁ to¹ hai₃ kom².
我 地 時 時 都 係 咁 .

7 Do you think (say) it is good to eat so late ?

Nei₂ wa₃ kom³ aan³ shik₄ faan₃ ho² m₁ ho² ni¹?
你 話 咁 晏 食 飯 好 唔 好 呢 .

8 Chinese are so, Westerners are about the same.

T'ong₁ yan₁ hai₃ kom², Sai¹ yan₁ to¹ hai₃ kom° sheung₃ *ha₃.
唐 人 係 咁, 西 人 都 係 咁 上 下 .

9 Do they live to be as old as Westerners ?

M₁ chi¹ k'ui₂ tei₃ nin₁ sui³ yau₂ sai¹ yan₁ kom³ toh¹ mo₂
ni¹?　唔知佢地年歲有西人咁多冇呢.

10 Some Chinese say that there are very few old Europeans.

Yau₂ ti¹ t'ong₁ yan₁ wa₃, sai¹ yan₁ ho² shiu² yau₂ lo₂ yan₁.
有 啲 唐 人 話 西 人 好 少 有 老 人 .

11 I see some old Chinese, but not many.

Ngoh₂ kin³ yau₂ ti¹ t'ong₁ yan₁ hai₃ lo₂, taan₃ hai₃
mo₂ kom³ toh¹.　我見有啲唐人係老,但係冇咁多.

12 Young Chinese are numerous.

Hau₃ shaang¹ ke³ t'ong₁ yan₁ hai₃ toh¹.
後 生 嘅 唐 人 係 多

THE TWENTY-EIGHTH LESSON

第 二 十 八 課—Tai₃ i₃ shap₄ paat₀ foh³

1	肥	Fei₁—*Fat.*		
2	瘦	Shau³, sau³—*Thin, lean.*		
3	難	Naan₁—*Hard, difficult.* Naan₃—*Difficulties.*		
4	易	I₃ — *Easy,* yik₄, *to exchange, barter (deal with)*		
5	音	Yam¹—*Sound, voice.*		
6	硬	Ngaang₃—*Hard (substance).*		
7	厚	Hau₂—*Thick* Hau₃—*Virtuous*		
8	薄	Pok₄—*Thin.*		
9	河	Hoh₁—*River.*		
10	運	Wan₃ — *Movement, remove, transport.*		

1 个隻牛係肥唔係. Koh² cheko ngau₁ hai₃ fei₁ m₁ hai₃?

1 Is that cow fat or not?

2 唔係，个隻牛係好瘦. M₁ hai₃, koh² cheko ngau₁ hai₃ ho² shau³.

2 No, that cow is very thin.

3 學唐話係唔係難呢. Hok₄ t'ong₁ *wa₃ hai₃ m₁ hai₃ naan₁ ni¹?

3 Is it difficult to learn Chinese or not?

4 唔係幾難用心學就易. M₁ hai₃ kei² naan₁ yung₃ sam¹ hok₄ tsau₃ i₃.

4 Not very difficult, if you use your mind it is easy.

5 講唐話娶好口音至講得好. Kong² t'ong₁ *wa₃ iu³ ho² hau² yam¹ chi kong² tak⁴ ho².

5 In speaking Chinese one must have good enunciation to be able to speak well.

6 唔好食硬野. M₁ ho' shik₄ ngaang₃ ye₃.

6 Do not eat hard things.

7 天熱娶厚衫唔娶呢. T'in¹ it₄ iu³ hau₂ shaan¹ m₁ iu³ ni¹?

7 Do you need a thick coat in hot weather.

8 唔娶，天熱我要薄衫，天冷至娶厚衫. M₁ iu³, t'in¹ it₄ ngoh₂ iu³ pok₄ shaam¹, t'in¹ laang₂ chi³ iu³ hau₂ shaam¹.

8 No, in hot weather I need thin clothes, only in cold weather I need thick clothes.

9 河水多數係淺嘅. Hoh₁ shui² toh¹ sho³ hai₃ ts'in² ke⁵.

9 Rivers are mostly shallow.

10 中國有條運河. Chung¹ kwok₀ yau₂ t'iu₁ wan₃ hoh₁.

10 There is a Canal in China.

The Twenty-eighth Exercise—(Conversation.)

1 Good morning, are you well to-day?

Kom³ tso² shan₁, kam¹ yat₄ ho² a¹? 咁早晨,今日好吖.

2 Yes, thanks, (I hope) you are well?

Ho²a⁵, yau₂ sam¹, sin¹ shaang¹ ho²? 好呀,有心,先生好.

3 Thank you. To-day we will go for a walk in the street and talk as we go.

Yau₂ sam,¹ kam¹ yat₄ t'ung₁ neiz hui³ kaai¹, ngob₂ tei₃ yat⁴ lo₃ haang₁ yat⁴ lo₃ kong²

有心,今日同你去街,我哋一路行一路講.

4 Good, what shall we talk about?

Ho² a¹, kong² mat⁴ ye₂ ho² ni¹? 好吖,講乜野好呢.

5 Shall we talk about men (good or not)?

Kong² yan₁ ho² m₁ ho² ni¹? 講人好唔好呢.

6 Good, what is it good to say about men?

Ho², yan₁ yau₂ mat⁴ ye₂ ho² kong² ni¹? 好,人有乜野好講呢.

7 A few days ago we talked about food. to-day we will talk about man's body.

Sin¹ kei² yat₄ kong² shik₄, kam¹ yat₄ kong² yan₁ ke³ shan¹. 先幾日講食,今日講人嘅身.

8 Is it better to eat much or little?

Shik₄ toh¹ ho² teng₃ shik₄ shiu² ho² ni¹? 食多好定食少好呢.

9 If you eat more you are fatter; if you eat less you are thinner; is that so?

Shik₄ toh¹ ti¹ fei₁ ti¹, shik₄ shiu² ti¹ shau³ ti¹; hai₃ m₁ hai₃ ni¹? 食多啲肥啲,食少啲瘦啲;係唔係呢.

10 Some people eat a great deal but they are thin. Some eat very little yet they are very fat.

Yau₂ ti¹ yan¹ shik₄ ho² toh¹, taan₃ hai₃ ho² shau³, yau₂ ti¹ yan₁ shik₄ ho² shiu², taan₃ hai₃ ho² fei₁. 有啲人食好多,但係好瘦,有的人食好少,但係好肥.

11 So, each of them is different. some eat and are not well.

Kom² ke⁵, kok₀ yau₂ kok₀ m₁ t'ung₁, yau₂ ti¹ yan₁ shik₄ to¹ m₁ tak⁴ ho². 咁嘅,各有各唔同,有啲人食都唔得好.

12 Why are they not well if they have food?

Tim² kaai² yau₂ tak⁴ shik₄ to¹ m₁ ho² ni¹? 點解有得食都唔好呢.

13 It is well for one to be careful in food and drink.

Yan₁ yan₁ shik₄ chan¹ hai₃ iu³ siu² sam¹ chi³ ho². 人人食真係要小心至好.

A SHORT LIST OF CLASSIFIERS
OR NUMERATIVES.

1. 个 koh^3 used for men, and generally.
2. 隻 $chek_0$ used for animals, birds, boats, **some** parts of body.
3. 件 kin_3 used for matters of business, **objects, coats.**
4. 間 $kaan^1$ used for houses, buildings, **rooms.**
5. 條 $t'iu_1$ used for many long things, **road,** chain, fish, trousers.
6. 張 $cheung^1$ used for tables, chairs, **sheets of** paper, beds, carpets, knives, etc.
7. 塊 $faai^3$ used for slices of bread, **pieces of** cloth, wood, paper.
8. 幅 fuk^4 used for maps, pictures, walls, **pieces** of ground.
9. 封 $fung^1$ used for letters.
10. 口 hau^2 used for nails, pistols, men.
11. 駕 ka^3 used for carriages, cars.
12. 枝 chi^1 used for pens, pencils, masts, **bran-** ches, flags.
13. 場 $ch'eung_1$ used for battles, law cases, **matters,** business.
14. 文 $*man_1$ used for money, cash.
15. 粒 nap^4 used for grains, rice, sand, **pills.**
16. 部 po_3 used for books.
17. 把 pa^2 used for fans, umbrellas, knives, **and** articles that may be held.
18. 位 $*wai_2$ used for people.
19. 笪 $taat_0$ used for places, land.
20. 頂 $ting^2$ used for hats, sedan chairs.
21. 度 to_0 used for bridges, doors, rivers, **etc.**
22. 對 tui^8 used for pairs of things, **shoes,** scrolls, etc.
23. 陣 $chan_8$ used for time, wind, showers, **flashes.**

A SHORT LIST OF FINALS.

The characters used for these are mostly
made up for the purpose.

1. 呀 A^3 euphonic, is used in two different
tones.

2. 吖 a^1 emphatic.

3. 啫 or 喳 $\left\{ \begin{array}{c} che^1 \text{ or} \\ cha^1 \end{array} \right\}$ in different tones, implies limitation,
used for only.

4. 嘅 ke' euphonic.

5. kwa^3 implies doubt, probably, used in two
tones.

6. 喇 la^1 emphatic, sometimes imperative.

7. 哩 le^1 used in various tones, mostly eu-
phonic, sometimes emphatic.

8. 咯 lok_o (k) usually silent like loh^3 euphonic.

9. 嗎 ma^3 used in six tones, interrogative.

10. 咩 me^1 interrogative.

11. 麼 moh^1 used in six tones, interrogative.

12. 嗱 na_1 emphatic.

13. 呢 ne^1 used in five tones, emphatic.

14. 呢 ni^1 interrogative.

15. 嚩 poh^3 emphatic, used after loh^3.

16. 喎 woh_3 in three tones or wa in three tones, a
quotation.

香港・澳門雙城成長經典

66

again (further)	又 yau₃, 亦 yik₄, 再 tsoi³	
all	喊唪吟 haam₃ pa(ng)₃ laang₃	
all round (all directions)	週 圍 chau¹ wai₁	
although	雖 然 sui¹ in₁	
always	時 時 shi₁ shi₁, 常時 sheung₁ shi₁	
because	因 爲 yan¹ wai₃	
besides, further	而 且 i₁ ch'e², 又 yau₃	
blessing	福 fuk⁴	
boundary (class)	界 kaai³, (student class) 學界 hok₄ kaai³	
butterflies	蝴 蝶 oo₁ *tip₄	
cannot be helped	冇柰何 mo₂ noi₃ hoh₁	
cannot help	柰唔何 noi₃ m₁ hoh₁	
club	俱樂部 k'ui¹ lok₄ po₃ (H.K. Club)	
	新公司 san¹ kung¹ sz¹	
command, order	吩 咐 fan¹ foo³	
common, general	平 常 p'eng₁ sheung₁	
company	公 司 kung¹ sz¹	
complete, perfect	完 全 uen₁ ts'uen₁	
customs, manners	規 矩 kw'ai¹ kui², 風俗 fung¹ tsuk₄	
descendants	子 孫 tsz² suen¹	
discuss	斟 酌 cham¹ cheuk₀	
domestic animals	畜 牲 ch'uk⁴ shang¹	
effect, influence	影 响 ying² heung²	
establish set up, begin	設 立 ch'it₀ laap₄	
examination	考 試 haau² shi³	
examine	查 察 ch'a₁ ch'aat₀	
family	家 人 ka¹ yan₁	
fragments (small)	零 碎 leng₁, sui³	
frequently	時 常 shi₁ sheung₁	
glass	玻 璃 poh¹ *lei₁	
God	上 帝 sheung₃ tai³	
good morning	早 晨 tso² shan₁	
good order, in	妥 當 t'oh₂ tong³	

government 國 家 kwok_0 ka^1, 政府 ching^3 foo^2

if 如 果 ue_1 kwoh^2, 倘若 t'ong^2 yeuk_4

influence 感 動 kom^2 tung_3

Jesus 耶 穌 ye_1 so^1

king 皇 帝 wong_1 tai^3

like (seems) 似 乎 ts'z_2 oo_1 (foo_1)

material 材 料 ts'oi_1 liu_3

moment 一 陣 yat^4 chan_3

movement 運 動 wan_3 tung_3

myriad (10,000) 一 萬 yat^4 maan_3

needlework 針 黹 cham^1 chi^2

neighbour 隔 籬 kaak_0 lei_1

occasionally 內 中 noi_3 chung^1, 耐不耐 noi_3 pat^4 *noi_3

originally 本 來 poon^2 loi_1, 原本 uen_1 poon^2

or 嘅 pe_3, 或 waak_4, 定 ting_3, 呀 a_3 嗎 me_3

peaceful 安 樂 on^1 lok_4, 和平 woh_1 p'eng_1

perfect 完 全 uen_1 ts'uen_1

perhaps 或 者 waak_4 che^2

police station 差 館 ch'aai^1 koon^2, 警局 king^2 *kuk_4

politics 政 治 ching^3 chi_3

prepare 預 備 ue_3 pei_3

reason, a 緣 故 uen_1 koo^3, 原因 uen_1 yan^1

regard as 以 爲 i_2 wai_1

sacrifice (self) 犧 牲 hei^1 shang^1

school 學 校 hok_4 haau_3, 書館 shue^1 koon^2

self 自 己 tsz_3 kei^2

sing songs 唱 歌 ch'eung^3 koh^1

students 學 生 hok_4 shang^1

study 研 究 in_1 kau^3, 學 hok_4

therefore 所 以 shoh^2 i_2

universal }
(general) } 普 通 p'o^2 t'ung^1

we, this and that 彼 此 pei^2 ts'z^2

THE TWENTY NINTH LESSON

第 二 十 九 課—Tai$_3$ i$_3$ shap$_4$ kau^2 foh^3

1	肚	T'o$_2$—Stomach.	6	耳	I$_2$—Ear, Ears.
2	餓	Ngoh$_1$—Hungry.	7	牙	Nga$_1$—Tooth, teeth.
3	眼	Ngaan$_2$—Eyes	8	指	Chi^2—Fingers, refer to, point.
4	瞓	Fan^3—Sleep.	9	自	Tsz$_3$—From, self.
5	痛	T'ung^2—Painful.	10	已	Kei^2—Self.

---

1 我食野落肚 Ngoh$_2$ shik$_4$ ye$_2$ lok$_4$ t'o$_2$.

2 食咗野肚唔餓 Shik$_4$ choh^2 ye$_2$ t'o$_2$ m$_1$ ngoh$_3$.

3 你隻眼見乜野呢 Nei$_2$ chek$_0$ ngaan$_2$ kin^3 mat^4 ye$_2$ ni^1?

4 我兩晚都唔瞓得，今晚見好眼瞓 Ngoh$_2$ leung$_2$ maan$_2$ to^1 m$_1$ fan^3 tak$_4$ kam^1 maan$_2$ kin^3 ho^2 ngaan$_2$ fan^3.

5 你眼有冇見痛 Nei$_2$ ngaan$_2$ yau$_2$ mo$_2$ kin^3 t'ung^1.

6 唔係，我兩隻耳見痛係真嘅 M$_1$ hai$_3$, Ngoh$_2$ leung$_2$ chek$_0$ i$_2$ kin^3 t'ung^3 hai$_3$ chan^1 ke^3.

7 呢幾日，有牙痛冇 Ni^1 kei^2 yat$_4$ yau$_2$ ngai$_1$ t'ung^3 mo$_2$?

8 你哋手指好番未 Nei$_2$ ti^1 shau^2 chi^2 ho^2 faan^1 mei$_3$.

9 我自前日見痛，今日好番 Ngoh$_2$ tsz$_3$ ts'in$_1$ yat$_4$ kin^3 t'ung^3, kam^1 yat$_4$ ho^2 faan^1.

10 我自己話，老人係咁，手脚或耳，時時有一樣痛. Ngoh$_2$ tsz$_3$ kei^2 wa$_3$, lo$_2$ yan$_1$ hai$_3$ kom^2, shau^2 keuk$_0$ wak$_4$ i$_2$ shi$_1$ shi$_1$ yau$_2$ yat^4 yeung^3 t'ung^1.

1 My food goes into my stomach.

2 After eating one is not hungry.

3 What is the matter with your eyes?

4 I have not slept well for two nights and my eyes are very sleepy this evening.

5 Do your eyes feel sore.

6 No, but really my ears are painful.

7 These few days have you had tooth ache?

8 Is your finger well yet?

9 For the last two days I have had pain, but to-day I am well.

10 I myself say, old people are so, either their hands or feet or ears are always sore.

The Twenty-ninth Exercise—(Conversation.)

1 Good morning, Why have I not seen you the last few days?

Tso² shan₁, tim² kaai² ni¹ kei² yat₄ mo₂ kin³ nei₂?

早晨點解呢幾日冇見你

2 These few days I have not been very well.

Ngoh₂ ni¹ kei² yat₄ m₁ hai₅ kei² ho².

我呢幾日唔係幾好.

3 What is the matter? Have you eaten too much?

Yau₂ mat⁴ sz₃ ni¹? Hai₃ shik₄ tak⁴ toh¹ kwoh³ t'au₁ m₁ hai₃?

有乜事呢,係食得多過頭唔係.

4 It is partly that. I ate too much and had stomach ache.

Yau₂ shiu² shiu² hai₃, ngoh₂ shik₄ tak⁴ toh¹ kwoh³ t'au₁, tsau₃ t'o₂ t'ung³. 有少少係,我食得多過頭,就肚痛.

5 Why did you not listen (attend) to what we said about eating?

Tim² kaai² koh² yat₄ kong² shik₄ nei₂ m₁ t'eng¹ ni¹?

點解个日講食你唔聽呢

6 That evening I was asked to a feast. The things were most excellent and I ate a good deal.

Koh² maan₂ yau₂ yan₁ kiu³ ngoh₂ hui³ yam², ti¹ ye₂ m₁ chi¹ kei² ho² shik₄, ngoh₂ shĭk₄ ho² toh¹.

个晚有人叫我去飲,啲野唔知幾好食,我食好多.

7 Why did you eat so much?

Tim² kaai² nei₂ shik₄ kom³ toh¹ ni¹? 點解你食咁多呢.

8 Need that be told? Every one, seeing good food, always eats and eats too much

Chung₃ shai² kong² *ke³, yan₁ yan₁ kin³ ye₂ ho² shik₄, shi₁ shi₁ to¹ hai₃ yat⁴ shik₄, shik₄ toh¹ kwoh³ t'au₁.

重使講嘅,人人見野好食,時時都係一食,食多過頭.

9 Why are you so foolish?

Tim² kaai² nei₂ kom³ mo₂ kin³ shik⁴ ni¹?

點解你咁冇見識呢.

10 I do not know. Really it may be said that I am foolish.

Ngoh₂ to¹ m₁ chi¹ to³, chan¹ hai₃ wa₃ tak⁴ mo₂ kin³ shik⁴ lok₀. 我都唔知到,真係話得冇見識略.

11 If you know you are foolish, what will you do?

Nei₂ chi¹ nei₂ mo₂ kin¹ shik⁴, nei₂ iu³ tim² *yeung₇?

你知你冇見識你要點樣.

12 Being foolish, one must give one's mind to study, that is it.

Mo₂ kin³ shik⁴ tsau, yung₃ sam¹ hok₄, ye₂ hai₃ la¹.

冇見識就用心學野係喇

香港·澳門雙城成長經典

THE THIRTIETH LESSON

第 三 十 課—Tai₃ saam¹ shap₄ foh³

1	苦	Foo³—*Bitter, pain, grief.*	6	懶	Laan₂—*Lazy.*
2	辛	San¹—*Pungent, acrid.*	7	惰	Toh₃—*Reluctant, slow.*
3	力	Lik₄—*Strength.*	8	蠢	Ch'un²—*Foolish.*
4	勤	K'an₁—*Industrious.*	9	精	Tsing¹—*Smart, energetic, energy.*
5	勢	Shai³—*Power, conditions.*	10	神	Shan₁—*Spirit, energy.*

1 佢見口苦,都見口乾. K'ui₂ kin¹ hau² foo², to¹ kin⁵ hau² kon¹.

1 His mouth is bitter, and also dry.

2 佢見得好辛苦. K'ui₂ kin³ tak⁴ ho² san¹ foo².

2 He has much pain.

3 佢係唔係冇力呢. K'ui₂ hai₃ m₁ hai, mo₂ lik₄ ni¹?

3 Has he no strength?

4 唔係,佢好勤力. M₁ hai₃, k'ui₂ ho² k'an₁ lik₄.

4 No, he is very industrious, (hard working).

5 舊時有个人好大勢力. Kau₃ shi₁ yau₂ koh³ yan₁ ho² taai₃ shai³ lik₄.

5 Formerly there was a man, who had great power.

6 佢係懶做工唔係. K'ui₂ hai₃ laan₂ tso₃ kung¹ m₁ hai₃?

6 Is he lazy (at work)?

7 係,佢好懶惰嘅. Hai₃, k'ui₂ ho² laan₂ toh₃ ke³.

7 Yes, he is very lazy.

8 點解佢咁蠢呢. Tim² kaai² k'ui₂ kom° ch'un² ni¹?

8 Why is he so foolish?

9 佢重話好精. K'ui₂ chung₃ wa₃ ho² tsing¹?

9 Yet he says (he is) very smart.

10 冇精神唔做得工. Mo₂ tsing¹ shan₁ m₁ tso₃ tak⁴ kung¹.

10 (If) one has no energy one cannot work.

The Thirtieth Exercise—(Conversation.)

1 To-day I am really feeling unwell.

Kam¹ yat₄ chan¹ hai₃ san¹ foo². 今日真係辛苦

2 Why are you so-ill (painful)?

Tim² kaai² kom⁵ san¹ foo² ni¹? 點解咁辛苦呢

3 Yesterday I told you the reason.

Tsok₄ yat₄ ngoh₂ wa₇ choh² nei₂ chi¹ tim² kaai² lok₀

昨 日 我 話 嘅 你 知 點 解 咯

4 What, you ate too much and you are not even better now. Is that so?

Mat⁴a³, shik₄ ye₂ toh¹ kwoh⁵ t'au₁, chung₅ mei₃ ho² faan¹, hai₃ m₁ hai₅ ni¹?

乜呀, 食野多過頭, 重未好番, 係唔係呢.

5 Yes, certainly, up to the present I am not yet well.

Hai₁, *ting₅ lok₀, to¹ mei₃ ho² faan¹

係 定 咯, 都 未 好 番

6 So hard to get well; What did you eat that day?

Kom³ naan₁ ho² ke³, nei₂ koh² yat₄ shik₄ ti¹ mat⁴ ye₂ ni¹? 咁 難 好 嘅, 你 个 日 食 啲 乜 野 呢

7 I have told you I ate a great many things.

To¹ wa₇ shik₄ ho² toh¹ ye₂ lok₀. 都話食好多野咯

8 Can you tell me how many things you ate?

Kong² tak⁴ ngoh₂ t'eng¹ nei₂ shik₄ kei² toh¹ ye₂ m₁ ni¹?

講 得 我 聽 你 食 幾 多 野 唔 呢

9 I can not tell you how many things I ate.

Shik₄ choh² kong² m₁ ch'ut⁴ kom³ toh¹.

食 嘅 講 唔 出 咁 多

10 I do not think you are sick. It is but laziness.

Ngoh₂ t'ai² nei₂ m₁ hai₅ yau₂ sz₅, pat⁴ kwoh⁵ laan₂ toh₃

我 睇 你 唔 係 有 事, 不 過 懶 惰

11 Am I lazy? I am very diligent. I really (have no energy).

Ngoh₂ laan₂ toh₃ a¹? Ngoh₂ ho² k'an₁ lik₄ ke³, mo₂ tsing¹ shan₁ tsau₅ hai₅ chan¹.

我懶惰吖! 我好勤力嘅, 有精神就係真

12 Diligence is good, do not be lazy. (practice laziness).

K'an₁ lik₄ hai₃ ho², m₁ ho² hok₄ laan₂ toh₂.

勤 力 係 好, 唔 好 學 懶 惰

THE THIRTY FIRST LESSON

第 三 十 一 課—Tai₃ saam¹ shap₄ yat⁴ foh³.

1	醫 I¹—*Cure, doctor.*	6	險 Him²—*Dangerous, risk.*
2	病 Peng₅—*Sick, disease*	7	傷 Sheung¹—*Wound, injure.*
3	藥 Yeuk₄—*Medicine.*	8	咪 Mai₂—*Do not.*
4	死 Sz,² (see,² say²)—*Die, dead.*	9	聲 Sheng¹—*Sound, voice.*
5	危 Ngai₁—*Dangerous.*	10	氣 Hei²—*Breath, anger*

1 佢係醫生 K'ui₂ hai₃ i¹ shang¹.

1 He is a doctor.

2 病人要請醫生 Peng₅ yan₁ iu⁵ ts'ing² i¹ shang¹.

2 Sick people must send for a doctor to see them.

3 醫生時時俾好苦嘅藥水過病人飲 I¹ shang¹ shi₁ shi₁ pei⁴ ho² foo² ke⁸ yeuk₄ shui² kwoh⁵ peng₃ yan₁ yam².

3 The doctor always gives very bitter medicine to the patients to drink.

4 冇人想死嘅 Mo₂ yan₁ seung² sz² ke⁹.

4 No one wants to die.

5 佢嘅病係好危 K'ui₂ ke³ peng₃ hai₃ ho² ngai₁.

5 His condition is critical.

6 有啲病係好危險嘅 Yau₂ ti¹ peng₃ hai₃ ho² ngai₁ him² ke³.

6 Some diseases are very dangerous.

7 我見一个人喺街俾貨車車傷 Ngoh₂ kin³ yat⁴ koh⁹ yan₁ hai² kaai¹ pei² foh³ ch'e¹ ch'e¹ sheung¹.

7 I saw a man in the street injured by a motor lorry.

8 你咪俾病人傷心至好 Nei₂ mai₂ pei² peng₃ yan₁ sheung¹ sam¹ chi³ ho².

8 Do not allow sick people to be worried (that is best).

9 佢唔講得好大聲 K'ui₂ m₁ kong² tak⁴ ho² taai₃ sheng¹.

9 He cannot speak very loud.

10 你睇佢重有氣冇 Nei₂ t'ai² k'ui₂ chung₃ yau₂ hei³ mo₂.

10 You see whether he still has any breath.

The Thirty-first Exercise—(Conversation.)

1 Good morning, are you well (again) to-day?

Tso² shan₁, kam³ yat₄ ho² faan¹ mei, ni¹ ?

早 晨, 今 日 好 番 未 呢

2 I am not yet well. I still have to see the doctor, (need the doctor to see me).

Mei₃ ho² faan¹. chung₃ iu³ i¹ shang¹ t'ai² chi⁵ tak⁴.

未 好 番, 重 要 醫 生 睇 至 得

3 What! are you still taking medicine ?

Mat⁴, nei₂ chung₃ shik₄ yeuk₄?　也 你 重 食 藥

4 Yes, being sick, I must take medicine.

Hai₃ a¹, yau₂ peng₃ tsau₃ iu³ shik₄ yeuk₄.

係 吖, 有 病 就 要 食 藥

5 (If you) did not take (medicine) what would happen?

M₁ shik₄ tsau₃ tim² ni¹ ?　唔 食 就 點 呢

6 (If I) did not take medicine (I) would die.

M₁ shik₄ yeuk₄ tsau₃ sz² lok₀.　唔 食 藥 就 死 咯

7 You cannot die so soon. Do you say you are in a critical condition? (Is that so)?

M₁ sz² tak⁴ kom³ faai³, nei₂ wa₃ ho² ngai₁, hai₃ m₁ hai₃ ni¹ ?　唔 死 得 咁 快, 你 話 好 危, 係 唔 係 呢.

8 It may not be very serious, If I were ill I could not walk, but I am still not out of danger.

M₁ hai₃ yat⁴ teng₃　ke³, ngai₁, tsau₃ m₁ haang₁ tak⁴ lok₀, taan₃ hai₃ to¹ yau₂ him².

唔 係 一 定 嘅. 危 就 唔 行 得 咯, 但 係 都 有 險.

9 What danger is there? You are not injured.

Ngai₁ him² mat⁴ ye₂? Nei₂ mo₂ shau₃ sheung¹ a¹ ?

危 險 乜 野, 你 冇 受 傷 吖.

10 Well, injured, I am not injured, do not talk so much.

Sheung¹, mo₂ mat⁴ sheung¹. mai₂ kong² kom³ toh¹.

傷 冇 乜 傷, 咪 講 咁 多

11 You are really long winded.

Nei₂ chan¹ hai₃ ch'eung₁ hei³. 你 真 係 長 氣.

12 I am not long-winded (tedious).

Ngoh₂ m₁ hai₃ ch'eung₁ hei³ a¹. 我 唔 係 長 氣 吖.

THE THIRTY-SECOND LESSON

第 三 十 二 課—Tai$_3$ saam^1 shap$_4$ i$_3$ foh^3

1	巾	Kan^1 — *Towel, handkerchief.*	6	除	Ch'ui$_1$ or ch'ue$_1$ — *Take off or away.*
2	毛	Mo$_1$—*Hair, hairy.*	7	衣	I^1—*Clothes.*
3	毡	Chin^1—*Blanket, felt.*	8	服	Fuk$_4$—*Serve, submit, I^1 fuk$_4$, clothes.*
4	帽	*Mo$_3$—*Hat.*	9	櫃	*Kwai$_3$— *Coffer, chest.*
5	擦	Ch'aat$_0$—*Brush, rub*	10	床	Ch'ong$_1$—*Bed*

1 搵一條手巾仔嚟俾我.
Ning^1 yat^4 t'iu$_0$ shau^2 kan^1 tsai^2 lai$_1$ pei^2 ngoh$_2$.

1 Bring me a handkerchief.

2 我要毛巾洗面. Ngoh$_2$ iu^3 mo$_1$ kan^1 sai^4 min$_3$.

2 I want a towel to wash my face.

3 今晚好熱我唔要毡.
Kam^1 *maan$_2$ ho^2 it$_4$ ngoh$_2$ m$_1$ iu^3 chin^1.

3 It is very hot to-night. I do not want a blanket.

4 你搵我件毡帽去做乜野
Nei$_2$ ning^1 ngoh$_2$ kin$_3$ chin^1 *mo$_3$ hui^3 tso$_3$ mat^4 ye$_2$?

4 Why did you take my felt hat away.

5 我擰你件毡帽去擦.
Ngoh$_2$ ning^1 nei$_2$ kin$_3$ chin^1 *mo$_3$ hui^3 ch'aat$_0$.

5 I took your felt hat to be brushed.

6 熱過頭,我一定要除衫.
It$_4$ *kwoh^3 t'au$_1$ ngoh$_2$ yat^4 teng$_3$ iu^3 ch'ue$_1$ shaam^1.

6 It is too hot, I must take off my coat.

7 落雨个時 有雨衣唔使濕身.
Lok$_4$ ue$_2$ koh^2 shi$_1$, yau$_2$ ue$_2$ i^1 m$_1$ shai^2 shap^4 shan$_1$.

7 When it rains if one has a raincoat one will not get wet.

8 你擠我的衣服喺邊處.
Nei^2 chai^1 ngoh$_2$ ti^1 i^1 fuk$_4$ hai^2 pin^1 shue^3.

8 Where did you put my clothes?

9 我擠你的衣服喺櫃.
Ngoh$_2$ chai^1 nei$_2$ ti^1 i^1 fuk$_4$ hai^2 kwai$_3$.

9 I put your clothes in the wardrobe.

10 真係眼瞓咯, 我想卽時去床瞓?
Chan^1 hai$_3$ ngaan$_2$ fan^3 lok$_0$, ngoh$_2$ seung^2 tsik^4 shi$_1$ hui^3 ch'ong$_1$ fan^3.

10 I am really sleepy, I want to go to bed at once.

The Thirty-second Exercise—(Conversation.)

1 What did you buy when you went out yesterday?

Tsok, vat, nei₂ hui³ kaai¹ maai₂ mat⁴ ye₂?

昨日你去街買乜野.

2 I went to buy some towels.

Ngoh₂ hui³ maai₂ ti¹ mo₁ kan¹. 我去買的毛巾.

3 Did you buy anything else?

Chung, yau₂ maai₂ mat⁴ ye₂ mo₂? 重有買乜野冇.

4 Yes, I bought a felt hat.

Yau₂, ngoh₂ maai₂ choh² yat⁴ kin₃ chin¹ *mo₃.

有，我買嘅一件毡帽.

5 Felt hats are not very good, one must always brush them, and always take off one's hat.

Chin¹ *mo₃ m₁ hai₃ kei² ho², iu³ shi₁ shi₁ ch'aat₀, shi₁ shi₁ ch'ui₁ *mo₃. 毡帽唔係幾好, 要時時擦, 時時除帽

6 Where do you put your clothes?

Nei₂ ti¹ i¹ fuk₄ chai¹ pin¹ shue³? 你的衣服擠邊處.

7 I put them in the wardrobe.

Ngoh₂ chai¹ hai² kwai₃. 我擠喺櫃

8 In which wardrobe did you put them?

Chai¹ hai² pin¹ koh³ kwai₃. 擠喺邊个櫃

9 In the large wardrobe near the bed.

Hai² ch'ong₁ pin¹ koh² koh³ taai₃ kwai₃.

喺床邊个个大櫃

10 Why can I not open the door of the wardrobe?

Tim² kaai² kwai₃ moon₁ m₁ hoi¹ tak⁴ ke³? 點解櫃門唔開得嘅

11 I could open it just now.

Ngoh₂ sin¹ t'au₁ to¹ hoi¹ tak⁴. 我先頭都開得.

12 Really I cannot open it.

Ngoh₂ chan¹ hai₃ m₁ hoi¹ tak⁴. 我真係唔開得.

THE THIRTY THIRD LESSON

第 三 十 三 課—Tai₃ saam¹ shap₄ saam¹ foh³

1	晒	Shaai⁶—*Dry in the sun.*	6	洋	Yeung₁—*Ocean, foreign.*
2	搣	K'aai₂—*Carry take, bring.*	7	皮	*P'ei₁—*Skin, leather, fur.*
3	遮	Che¹—*Shade, shelter umbrella.*	8	鞋	Haai₁—*Shoes.*
4	抹	Maat₀ or moot₀—*Wipe, dust.*	9	熨	T'ong³—*To iron.*
5	鏡	Keng⁵—*Mirror, Looking-glass*	10	斗	Tau²—*A measure, Vessel.*

1. 點解你个面晒得咁黑呢? Tim² kaai' nei₂ koh³ min₃ shaai' tak⁴ kom³ hak⁴ ni¹?
   Why is your face so dark?

2. 佢搣的紙嚟寫字 K'ui₂ k'aai₂ ti¹ chi² lai₁ se₂ tsz₂.
   He used the paper to write on.

3. 你要用帽至得, 唔係要用遮 Nei₂ iu yung₃ mo₃ chi tak', m₁ hai₃ iu⁹ yung₃ che.¹
   You must wear a hat If not, you must use an umbrella (instead of a hat.)

4. 我去街買布抹檯 Ngoh₂ hui³ kaai¹ maai₂ po³ maat₀ *t'oi₁.
   I went out to buy some cloth for dusting the table.

5. 你唔睇吓个鏡 Nei₂ m₁ t'ai² ha₂ koh³ keng⁵?
   Why do you not look in a glass.

6. 有人話洋貨好 Yau₂ yan₁ wa₁ yeung₁ foh³ ho².
   Some people say foreign goods are good.

7. 今日你嘅皮黑嘅略 Kam¹ yat₁ nei₂ ke' p'ei₁ hak⁴ choh² lok₂.
   To-day your skin is quite dark.

8. 一定冇皮鞋咁黑 Yat⁴ teng₃ mo₂ p'ei₁ haai₁ kom³ hak⁴.
   It is certainly not so black as boots.

9. 呢件衫要熨至得, 你用乜嚟熨呢 Ni¹ kin₃ shaam₁ iu⁹ t'ong⁹ chi³ tak', nei₂ yung₃ mat' ye₂ t'ong³ ni¹?
   This coat must be ironed. What will you use to iron it?

10. 用電熨斗係快的 Yung₃ tin₂ t'ong¹ tau² hai₃ faai⁶ ti¹.
    It is quicker to use an electric iron.

The Thirty-third Exercise—(Conversation)

1 Why is your face so red to day?

Kam¹ yat₄ nei₂ koh³ min₃ tso₃ mat⁴ kom³ hung₁ ni¹?

今日你個面做乜咁紅呢.

2 Yes, I have just drunk a great deal.

Hai₅, ngoh₂ tsau₃ chi³ vam² ho² toh¹.

係，我就至飲好多.

3 How much did you drink?

Yam² tak⁴ kei² toh¹ ni¹? 飲得幾多呢.

4 I drank a great deal and as I drank I kept wiping my face with a handkerchief.

Yam²ho² toh¹, yat⁴ lo₃ yam², yat⁴ lo₃ yung₃ shau² kau¹ maat₀ min₃. 飲好多，一路飲，一路用手巾抹面.

5 Then it would certainly be red. I think you must have been in the sun.

Kom² tsau₃ yat⁴ teng₃ hung₁ lok₀, ngoh₂ t'ai² yau₂ it₄ *t'au₁ shaai³ to¹ m̩ teng₃.

咁就一定紅咯，我睇有熱頭晒都唔定.

6 I must look into a mirror.

Ngoh₂ iu³ yung₃ keng³ t'ai² ha₂. 我要用鏡睇吓.

7 Do you say it is as red as foreign cloth?

Nei₂ wa₃ hai₃ m̩ hai₃ yeung₁ po³ kom³ hung₁ ni¹?

你話係唔係洋布咁紅呢.

8 It is pretty red. The skin is red.

To¹ hai₁ kei² hung₁, ti¹ p'ei₁ hung₁ a³.

都係幾紅，啲皮紅呀.

9 One must not expose oneself to the sun, and make one's skin so black (dark).

To¹ hai₁ m̩ ho² shaai³ kom³ hak⁴ ke³.

都係唔好晒咁黑嘅.

10 Yes, without a hat one may be scorched to a black colour.

Hai₃ mo₂ *mo₃ stau₃ shaai³ tak⁴ ho² hak⁴.

係，冇帽就晒得好黑.

THE THIRTY-FOURTH LESSON

第 三 十 四 課—Tai₃ saam¹ shap₄ sz³ foh³

1	光 Kwong¹—*Light, bright.*	6	糟 Tso¹—*Residue, dregs*
2	鮮 Sin¹—*Fresh.*	7	換 Oon₃—*Change.*
3	試 Shi¹—*Try, test, examine.*	8	動 Tung₃—*Move, movement.*
4	靚 Leng³—*Pretty, beautiful.*	9	衞 Wai₃ — *Protect,* (Wai₃ shaang¹) *sanitary.*
5	污 Oo¹—*Dirty.*	10	合 Hop₄— *Right, exact, agree.*

1 電燈光過油燈. Tin₃ tang¹ kwong¹ kwoh⁸ yau₁ tang₃.
Electric lamps are brighter than oil lamps.

2 佢嘅衫熨得好光鮮. K'ui₂ ke³ shaam¹ t'ong³ tak⁴ ho² kwong¹ sin¹.
His coat is ironed very well (bright and fresh).

3 你試吓用電熨斗. Nei₂ shi⁰ ha₂ yung₃ tin₃ t'ong³ tau².
You try an electric iron.

4 真係熨得好靚. Chan¹ hai₃ t'ong³ tak⁴ ho² leng³.
Really it irons very well.

5 你嘅面有啲污點. Nei₂ ke³ min₃ yau₂ ti¹ oo¹ tim².
There are some dirty spots on your face.

6 係,真係好污糟. Hai₃, chan¹ hai₃ ho² oo¹ tso¹.
Yes, really it is very dirty

7 做乜你今朝唔換檯布呢 Tso₃ mat⁴ nei₂ kam¹ chiu¹ m₁ oon₃ *t'oi₁ po⁸ ni¹²?
Why did you not change the table cloth this morning?

8 我起身晏有時候運動. Ngoh₂ hei² shan¹ aan'mo₂ shi₁ hau wan₁ tung₃.
I got up late and did not have time for exercise.

9 地方冇衞生人就生病. Tei₃ fong¹ mo₂ wai₃ shaang¹ yan₁ tsau₃ shaang¹ peng₃
If the place is not sanitary people will get sick.

10 係吖, 唔合衞生就生病. Hai₃ a¹, m₁ hop₄ wai₃ shang¹ tsau₃ shaang¹ peng₃.
Yes, if the place is not sanitary, people will become sick

The Thirty-fourth Exercise—(Conversation.)

1 It is dawn. Get up.

T'in¹ kwong¹ lok₀, hei² shan¹ a¹.   天光咯, 起身吖

2 Well, to-day we must buy some thing fresh to eat.

Ho² a¹, kam¹ yat₄ iu³ maai₂ ti¹ san¹ sin¹ ye₂ shik₄.

好吖, 今日要買啲新鮮野食

3 Try to get a little veal for food.

Sh₁ ha₂ maai₂ ti¹ ngau₁ tsai² yuk₄ shik₄ ha₂.

試吓買啲牛仔肉食吓

4 All is useless (false), you must sweep the place clean.

Mat⁴ to¹ hai₃ ka², so³ tseng₃ ti¹ tei₃ fong¹ chi³ tak⁴.

乜都係假, 掃淨啲地方至得

5 All right, How nice your coat is ?

Tak⁴ lok₀, mat⁴ nei₂ kin₃ shaam¹ kom³ leng³ *ke³ ?

得 咯, 乜你件衫咁靚嘅

6 Yes, it is pretty good (bright and fresh). It is newly bought

To¹ hai₃ kei² kwong³ sin¹, hai₃ san¹ maai₂ ke³.

都係幾光鮮, 係新買嘅

7 It seems to me that you have ironed it.

Ngoh₂ t'ai² nei₂ pei² t'ong³ tau² t'ong² kwoh³.

我睇你俾熨斗熨過

8 Yes, how keen your eyes are !

Mat⁴ nei₂ kom³ ho² ngaan₂ ke³ !   乜你咁好眼嘅

9 That place is very dirty.

Koh¹ ti³ tei₃ fong¹ ho² oo¹ tso¹.   个啲地方好污糟

10 Yes. it is not healthy, you must sweep it.

Hai₃, ho² m₁ hop₄ wai₃ shaang¹. iu³ so³ kwoh³ chi³ tak³

係好唔合衞生, 要掃過至得

11 Yes, tell some one to come quickly and clean it.

Hai₃ lok₀, kiu³ yan₁ faai³ ti¹ lai₁ so³ la¹.

係咯, 叫人快啲嚟掃喇

12 Ah muk, go quickly and sweep the floor.

Ah¹ muk₄, nei₂ faai⁴ ti¹ hui³ so³ tei₃.

亞木, 你快啲去掃地

THE THIRTY-FIFTH LESSON

第 三 十 五 課—Tai₃ saam¹ shap₁ ng₂ foh'

1	會	Ooi₂—*Can, able, will*	6	臭	Ch'au'—*Foul, stinking.*
2	剃	T'ai³—*Shave, cut, dress hair.*	7	梘	Kaan²—*Soap*
3	鬚	So'—*Beard.*	8	香	Heung¹—*Fragrant.*
4	剪	Tsin²—*Cut with scissors, shear.*	9	頂	Teng²—*Top.*
5	髮	Faat₀—*Hair.*	10	籃	*Laam₁—*Basket.*

1	佢會嚟唔會？ K'ui₂ ooi₂ lai₁ m₁ ooi₂.	Will he come or not ?
2	你會剃頭唔會. Nei₂ ooi₂ t'ai³ t'au₁ m₁ ooi₂.	Can you dress hair ?
3	我唔會剃頭，我會剃鬚. Ngoh₂ m₁ ooi' t'ai t'au₁ ngoh₂ ooi₁ t'ai' so¹.	I cannot dress hair but I can shave my beard.
4	佢剪乜野呢. K'ui₂ tsin² mat⁴ ye₂ ni¹ ?	What is he cutting (with scissors) ?
5	佢剪髮. Kiu₂ tsin² faat₀.	He is cutting hair.
6	你洗頭係落臭水洗唔係 Nei₂ sai² t'au₁ hai₃ lok₄ ch'au³ shui² sai² m₁ hai₃.	Do you wash your head with disinfectant ?
7	唔係，我洗頭用梘洗. M₁ hai₃, ngoh₂ sai² t'au₁ yung₃ kaan² sai'.	No, I use soap to wash my head.
8	上等香梘好香. Sheung₂ tang² heung¹ kaan² ho² heung¹.	The best scented soap is very fragrant.
9	好多人揸臭水去山頂賣 Ho' toh¹ yan₁ ning¹ ch'au' shui² hui' shaan¹ teng⁴ maai₃.	Many people take disinfectant to the Peak to sell.
10	佢用籃揸去賣嘅. K'ui₂ yung₃ *laam₁ ning¹ hui' maai₃ ke'.	He carries it with basket (to sell).

The Thirty-fifth Exercise—(Conversation.)

1 What news is there to-day ?

Kam¹ yat₄ yau₂ mat⁴ san¹ *man₁ ?

今 日 有 乜 新 聞

2 There is, China is prepared for war.

Yau₂ a¹, chung¹ kwok₆ seung² ta².　有吟,中國想打

3 Why should China fight ?

Tim² kaai² iu⁹ ta² ni¹ ?　點 解 要 打 呢?

4 They say, they must fight.

Kui₂ tei₃ wa₃, m₁ ta² m₁ tak⁴.

佢 地 話, 唔 打 唔 得

5 Why do they all want to fight ?

Tim² kaai² k'ui₂ taai₃ chung³ iu³ ta² ni¹?

點 解 佢 大 衆 要 打 呢?

6 Will they certainly do so later ?

K'ui₂ tei₃ hau₃ loi₁ yat⁴ ting₃ iu³ kom° *yeung₃ tso₆ me¹?

佢 哋 後 來 一 定 要 咁 樣 做 (咩)

7 Some people say there will be no fighting soon.

Yau₂ yan₁ wa₃ mo₂ kei² *noi₃ tsau₃ mo₂ tak⁴ ta².

有 人 話 冇 幾 耐 就 冇 得 打

8 I also hope that they will not fight.

Ngoh₂ to¹ seung² k'ui₂ tei₃ m₁ ho² ta².

我 都 想 佢 哋 唔 好 打

9 The corpses on the battlefield smell very bad.

Ta² sz² ti¹ yan₁ ho² ch'au³ ke³.

打 死 的 人 好 臭 嘅

10 Yes, but after disinfecting them there is no offensive smell.

Hai, taan₃ hai₃ yung₃ yeuk₄ shui² tsau₃ m₁ ooi₂ ch'au³.

係, 但 係 用 藥 水 就 唔 會 臭

THE THIRTY SIXTH LESSON

第 三 十 六 課—Tai₉ saam¹ shap₄ luk₄ foh³

1	羊	Yeung₁—Sheep, goat.	6 晝	*Taan₃—an egg.
2	奶	Naai₂—Milk.	7 狗	Kau²—Dog.
3	猪	Chue¹—Pig.	8 貓	Maau¹—Cat.
4	骨	Kwat⁴—Bone.	9 鼠	Shue²—Rat.
5	雞	Kai¹—Fowl.	10 味	Mei₃—Flavour, taste.

1 你食羊肉唔食 Nei₂ shik₄ yeung₁ yuk₄ m₁ shik₄?

2 我食羊肉都飲牛奶 Ngoh₂ shik₄ yeung₁ yuk₄ to¹ yam¹² ngau₁ naai₂.

3 猪肉好食定牛肉好食呢 Chue¹ yuk₄ ho² shik₄ teng₃ ngau₁ yuk₄ ho² shik₄ ni¹?

4 牛肉好食,猪肉冇骨都係好食 Ngau₁ yuk₄ ho² shik₄, chue¹ yuk₃ mo₂ kwat⁴ to¹ hai₃ ho² shik₄.

5 雞肉係好食過牛肉 Kai¹ yuk₄ hai₃ ho² shik₄ kwoh³ ngau₁ yuk₄.

6 朝朝我食三隻雞蛋 Chiu¹ chiu¹ ngoh₂ shik₄ saam¹ chek₀ kai¹ *taan₃.

7 我屋企有一隻狗睇門口 Ngoh₂ uk⁴ k'ei¹² yau₂ yat⁴ chek₀ kau² t'ai² moon₁ hau².

8 前日佢買咞一隻三色貓 T'sin₁ yat₄ k'ui₂ maai₂ choh² yat⁴ chek₀ saam¹ shik⁴ maau¹.

9 貓噲食老鼠 Maau¹ ooi₂ shik₄ lo₂ shue².

10 雞肉真係好味 Kai¹ yuk₄ chan¹ hai₃ ho² mei₃.

1 Do you eat mutton?

2 I eat mutton and also drink cow's milk.

3 Is pork better to eat or beef?

4 Beef is good to eat, pork without bones is also good to eat.

5 Chicken is better to eat than beef.

6 Every morning I eat three eggs.

7 In my house I have a dog to watch the door.

8 The day before yesterday he bought a three coloured cat.

9 Cats are able to eat rats.

10 The flesh of fowls really tastes good.

The Thirty-sixth Exercise—(Conversation.)

1 Yesterday I bought three goats.

Tsok$_4$ yat$_4$ ngoh$_2$ maai$_2$ saam^1 chek$_0$ *yeung$_1$.

昨 日 我 買 三 隻 羊

2 Why did you buy them?

Maai$_2$ lai$_1$ tso$_3$ mat^4 ye$_2$ ni^1? 買 嚟 做 乜 野 呢

3 Having bought them I shall have goat's milk to drink.

Maai$_2$ choh^2 tak^4 yeung$_1$ naai$_2$ lai$_1$ yam^2.

買 咗 得 羊 奶 嚟 飲

4 Is goat's milk good to drink?

Yeung$_1$ naai$_2$ ho^2 yam^2 m$_1$ ni^1? 羊 奶 好 飲 唔 呢

5 Pretty good. Some people say it is better than cow's milk

Kei^2 ho^2 yam^2, yau$_2$ yan$_1$ wa$_3$ ho^2 yam^2 kwoh^3 ngau$_1$
naai$_2$. 幾 好 飲, 有 人 話 好 飲 過 牛 奶

6 Why does every one drink cow's milk, and not goat's milk?

Tim^2 kaai^2 yan$_1$ yan$_1$ yam^2 ngau$_1$ naai$_2$ m$_1$ yam^2 yeung$_1$
naai$_2$ ni^1? 點 解 人 人 飲 牛 奶 唔 飲 羊 奶 呢

7 I do not know why, but some people drink goat's milk.

Ngoh$_1$ m$_1$ chi^1 tim^2 kaai^2. taan$_3$ hai$_3$ to^1 yau$_2$ yan$_1$ yam^2
yeung$_1$ naai$_2$. 我 唔 知 點 解, 但 係 都 有 人 飲 羊 奶

8 (The customs of) all countries are different, Some people eat pork, some people eat dog's flesh.

Yat^4 *kwok$_0$ kwok$_0$ m$_1$ t'ung$_1$ ke^3, yau$_2$ yan$_1$ shik$_4$
chue^1 yuk$_4$, yau$_2$ yan$_1$ shik$_4$ kau^2 yuk$_4$.

一 國 國 唔 同 嘅, 有 人 食 猪 肉, 有 人 食 狗 肉

9 I have heard some people say that there are some men who eat rats.

Ngoh$_2$ t'eng^1 yan$_1$ kong^2, yau$_2$ yan$_1$ shik$_4$ lo$_2$ shue^2 to^1
yau$_2$. 我 聽 人 講, 有 人 食 老 鼠 都 有

10 I do not know whether they are good to eat or not. Eggs are better to eat than many things however.

M$_1$ chi^1 ho^2 shik$_4$ m$_1$ ho^2, taan$_3$ hai$_3$ kai^1 *taan$_3$ ho^2
shik$_4$ kwoh^3 ho^2 toh^1 yeung$_4$.

唔 知 好 食 唔 好, 但 係 雞 蛋 好 食 過 好 多 樣

THE THIRTY SEVENTH LESSON

第 三 十 七 課—Tai₃ saam¹ shap₄ ts'at¹ foh˙

1	餐	Ts'aan¹—*A Meal.*		6	刀	To¹—*Knife.*
2	湯	T'ong¹—*Soup.*		7	义	Ch'a¹—*Fork.*
3	羹	Kang¹—*Spoon.*		8	酒	Tsau²—*Wine.*
4	碟	Tip₄—*Plate.*		9	壺	Oo₁—*Pot.*
5	碗	Oon²—*Bowl.*		10	杯	Pui¹—*Cup.*

1 你幾點鐘食餐呢 Nei₂ kei² tim² chung¹ shik₄ ts'aan¹ ni¹?

1 When do you take your meal?

2 你食餐有飲湯冇呢 Nei₂ shik₄ ts'aan¹ yau₂ yam² t'ong¹ mo₂ ni¹?

2 When you eat your meal do you take soup?

3 有,我用羹嚟飲湯 Yau₂, ngoh₂ yung₄ kang¹ lai₁ yam² t'ong¹.

3 Yes, I use a spoon to take soup.

4 西人用碟食餐係唔係呢 Sai¹ yan₁ yung₃ tip₄ shik₄ ts'aan¹ hai₃ m₁ hai₃ ni¹?

4 Do Europeans use plates to serve their meals?

5 係,唐人用碗多,都有用碟 Hai₃, t'ong₁ yan₁ yung₃ oon² toh¹, to¹ yau₂ yung₃ tip₄.

5 Yes, Chinese mostly use bowls to eat their food, some also use plates.

6 西人用刀食肉係唔係呢 Sai¹ yan₁ yung₃ to¹ shik₄ yuk₄ hai₃ m₁ hai₃ ni¹?

6 Do Europeans use knives to cut meat (at meals?)

7 係,西人用刀叉 Hai₃, sai¹ yan₁ yung₃ to¹ ch'a¹.

7 Yes, Europeans use knives and forks to eat with.

8 你食飯有飲酒冇 Nei₂ shik₄ faan₃ yau₂ yam² tsau² mo₂?

8 When you eat rice do you drink wine?

9 茶壺大過酒壺 Ch'a₁ oc₁ taai₃ kwoh³ tsau² oc₁.

9 Teapots are larger than wine-pots.

10 西人飲酒用大水杯,唐人用細酒杯 Sai¹ yan₁ yam² tsau² yung₃ taai₃ shui² pui¹, t'ong¹ yan₁ yung₃ sai³ tsau² pui¹.

10 Europeans take wine with glasses, Chinese drink wine with small wine cups.

The Thirty-seventh Exercise—(Conversation.)

1 To-day it would be well to talk of eating.

Kam¹ yat₄ kong² ha₂ shik₄ to¹ ho² a¹

今 日 講 吓 食 都 好 吖

2 Very well, do Europeans and Chinese take their food in different ways?

Ho² a¹, Sai¹ yan₁ shik₄ ye₂ m₁ t'ung₁ t'ong₁ yan₁ hai₃
m₁ hai₃ ni¹ ? 好吖,西人食野唔同唐人係唔係呢

3 Yes, they are different in many ways.

Hai₃, ho² toh¹ ye₂ to¹ m₁ t'ung₁.

係, 好 多 野 都 唔 同

4 Europeans serve soup in plates.

Sai¹ yan₁ yam² t'ong¹ yung₃ *tip₄.

西 人 飲 湯 用 碟

5 Some people cannot distinguish whether the food they eat is good or bad.

Yau₂ ti¹ yan₁ shik₄ ye₂ to¹ m₁ chi¹ ti¹ ye₂ ho² m₁ ho².

有 啲 人 食 野 都 唔 知 啲 野 好 唔 好

6 He requires to drink a lot of water every day.

K'ui₂ yat₄ yat₄ iu⁵ yam² ho² toh¹ shui².

佢 日 日 要 飲 好 多 水

7 Does he take soup.

Yau₂ yam² t'ong¹ mo₂ ni¹ ? 有 飲 湯 冇 呢

8 Yes, he takes soup with a large spoon, he eats his meal with knives and forks.

Yau₂, k'ui₂ yam² t'ong¹ yung₃ taai³ kang¹, shik₄ ts'aan¹
yung₃ to¹ ch'a¹. 有,佢飲湯用大羹,食餐用刀叉

9 He drinks water and soup. Does he drink wine ?

Yam² shui² yam² t'ong¹, yau₂ yam² tsau² mo₂ ni¹ ?

飲 水 飲 湯, 有 飲 酒 冇 呢

10 Yes, he always drinks several large glasses of wine.

Yau₂, k'ui₂ shi₁ shi₁ yam² kei² taai₃ pui¹ tsau².

有, 佢 時 時 飲 幾 大 杯 酒

THE THIRTY-EIGHTH LESSON

第 . 三 十 八 課—Tai₃ saam¹ shap₄ paat₀ foh⁸

1	切 Ts'it₀—*Cut, mince.*	6	麥 Mak₄—*Wheat.*
2	餅 Peng²—*Cake.*	7	菓 Kwoh²—*Fruit.*
3	粉 Fan²—*Powder, flour,*	8	糖 T'ong₁—*Sugar.*
4	麵 Min₃—*Wheaten.*	9	鹽 Im₁—*Salt.*
5	飽 Paau¹—*Cake, bread.* Paau²—*Repletion.*	10	鹹 Haam₁—*Briny, salt taste.*

1 小心切至好,唔係噲切親手. Siu² sam¹ ts'it₀ chi³ ho², m₁ hai₃ ooi₂ ts'it₀ ts'an¹ shau². — One must be careful in cutting, or else one may cut one's hand.

2 邊個搋咁多餅嚟, Pin¹ koh³ ning¹ kom³ toh¹ peng² lai₁ ? — Who brought so many cakes here?

3 呢啲係乜野粉. Ni¹ ti¹ hai₃ mat⁴ ye₂ fan² ? — What kind of powder is this ?

4 个啲係麵粉. Koh² ti¹ hai₃ min₃ fan². — That is wheaten flour.

5 麵粉要嚟整麵飽. Min₃ fan² iu³ lai₁ ching² min₃ paau¹, — Flour is used to make bread.

6 今朝我食咗一大碗牛奶麥粉. Kam¹ chiu¹ ngoh₂ shik₄ choh² yat⁴ taai₃ oon' ngau₁ naai₂ mak₄ fan². — This morning I ate a large bowl of oatmeal and milk.

7 人人都話生菓係好食. Yan₁ yan₁ to¹ wa₃ shaang¹ kwoh² hai ho² shik₄. — Everyone says fresh fruit is good to eat.

8 食糖菓唔使落糖. Shik₄ t'ong₁ kwoh² m₁ shai² lok₄ t'ong₁. — One need not add sugar to jam when eating it.

9 个啲湯冇味嘅,我要落鹽. Koh₂ ti¹ tong¹ mo₂ mei₃ ke³, ngoh₂ iu³ lok₄ im₁. — That soup is tasteless, I want to add salt to it.

10 唔好落咁多鹽唔係噲鹹過頭. M₁ ho² lok₄ kom³ toh¹ im₁ m₁ hai₃ ooi₂ haam₁ kwoh₃ t'au₁. — Do not put in so much salt, or it will be too briny.

The Thirty-eighth Exercise—(Conversation.)

1. Are there any other differences between Europeans and Chinese in ways of taking food ?

   Sai¹ yan₁ t'ung₁ t'ong₁ yan₁ shik₄ ye₂ chung₃ yau, mat⁴ fan¹ pit₄ ni¹?

   西人同唐人食野重有乜分別呢

2. Yes, a great many. I have heard some people say they differ in many ways.

   Yau₂, ho² toh¹, ngoh₂ t'eng¹ yan₁ kong² koh² ti¹ ye₂ tsau₅ ho² toh¹ m₁ t'ung₁.

   有好多,我聽人講个啲野就好多唔同

3. What are the differences ?

   Tim² *yeung₃ m₁ t'ung₁ ni¹?   點樣唔同呢

4. We eat rice whilst they eat bread cutting it into slices.

   Ngoh₂ tei₃ shik₄ faan₅, k'ui₂ toi₅ shik₄ min₃ paau¹, ts'it₀ hoi¹ yat⁴ *faai⁸ faai⁸ shik₄.

   我哋食飯,佢哋食麵飽,切開一塊塊食

5. What else ?

   Chung₃ yau₂ ni¹?   重 有 呢

6. It is more than I can tell. We use bowls. They mostly use plates.

   M₁ kong² tak⁴ kom³ toh¹, ngoh₂ tei₃ yung₃ oon², k'ui₂ tei₃ yung₃* tip₄ toh¹.

   唔 講 得 咁 多, 我 哋 用 碗, 佢 哋 用 碟 多

7. They eat porridge. Is that good or not ?

   K'ui₂ tei₃ shik₄ mak₄ fan² ho² m₁ ho² ni¹?

   佢 哋 食 麥 粉 好 唔 好 呢

8. It is good. Many Chinese also eat oatmeal (porridge).

   Ho², t'ong₁ yan₁ ho² toh¹ to' shik₄ mak₄ fan².

   好, 唐 人 好 多 都 食 麥 粉

9. Do the Chinese eat porridge with sugar or salt ?

   T'ong₁ yan₁ shik₄ mak₄ fan² lok₄ t'ong₁ teng₃ lok₄ im₁ ni¹?

   唐 人 食 麥 粉 落 糖 定 落 鹽 呢

10. It depends upon what they like, sometimes they add sugar and sometimes salt.

    Mo₂ yat⁴ teng₃ ke³, yau₂ shi₁ lok₄ t'ong₁ yau₂ shi₁ lok₄ im₁.   冇一定嘅有時落糖有時落鹽

THE THIRTY NINTH LESSON

第 三 十 九 課--Tai₃ saam¹ shap, kaau² foh'

1	機	Kei¹—*Machine, loom.*	6	向 Heung³—*Towards, direction, formerly.*
2	器	Hei³—*Vessel, utensil, apparatus.*	7	停 T'ing₁—*Stop.*
3	飛	Fei¹—*To fly.*	8	壞 Waai₃—*Destroy, damage.*
4	搭	Taap₀—*To take passage.*	9	尾 Mei₂—*Tail, end.*
5	站	Chaam₃—*A station.*	10	擺 Paai²—*Spread out, move.*

1 呢啲係乜野機呢 Ni¹ ti¹ hai₃ mat⁴ ye₂ kei¹ ni¹?

2 个啲係機器 Koh²_ti¹ hai₃ kei¹ hei³.

3 係飛機唔係 Hai₃ fei¹ kei¹ m₁ hai;.

4 唔係你想搭飛機唔想呢 M₁ hai₃, nei₂ seung² taap, fei¹ kei¹ m₁ seung² ni¹?

5 想嘅,但唔知有站有呢 Seung² ke³, taan₃ m₁ chi¹ yau₂ chaam₃ mo₂ ni¹?

6 飛機向站落要細心 飛近站就要慢車 Fei¹ kei¹ heung₃ chaam₃ lok₄, iu⁹ sai³ sam¹, fei¹ kan₃ chaam₃ tsau⁸ iu³ maan₃ ch'e¹.

7 到站停車,但有个站唔停車 To³ chaam₃ t'ing₁ ch'e¹, taan₃ yau₂ koh° chaam₃ m₁ t'ing₁ ch'e¹.

8 車壞必要停車嚟整好 Ch'e¹ waai₃ pit⁴ iu⁵ t'ing₁ ch'e¹ lai₁ ching² ho².

9 車尾有紅燈 Ch'e¹ mei₂ yau₂ hung₁ tang¹.

10 車尾兩頭擺,就好危險略 Che¹ mei₂ leung₂ t'au¹ paai², tsau₃ ho² ngai₁ him² lok₀.

1 What kind of machine is this?

2 That is an engine.

3 Is it a flying machine?

4 No, do you wish to ride in an aeroplane?

5 I wish to, but do not know whether there are any stations.

6 Aeroplanes approaching a station must descend carefully, when near the aerodrome they must go slowly.

7 A station being reached, the train stops. It, however, does not stop at all stations

8 If the engine is out of order it must be stopped and repaired.

9 At the rear of the train there is a red light.

10 A violent swing at the rear of a train is very dangerous,

The Thirty-ninth Exercise—(Conversation.)

1 I have not seen you for a long time. Where have you been?

M₁ kin³ kom³ noi₃, nei₂ hui³ pin¹ shue³?

唐 見 咁 耐, 你 去 邊 處

2 I have been to Shanghai.

Ngoh₂ hui⁵ sheung₅ hoi². 我 去 上 海

3 How do you go to Shanghai, can you go there by train?

Hui¹ sheung₅ hoi² tim² hui³ ni¹? Yau₂ foh² ch'e¹ hui³ mo₂ ni¹? 去上海點去呢?有火車去冇呢?

4 No, one must go by steamer, sometimes aeroplanes are also available.

Mo₂ iu³ ts'ol₂ foh² shuen₁. nei₃ chung¹ to¹ yau₂ fei¹ kei¹.

冇, 要 坐 火 船, 內 中 都 有 飛 機.

5 Are there stations for aeroplanes?

Fei¹ kei¹ yau₂ mo₂ chaam₃ ni¹? 飛 機 有 冇 站 呢

6 Sometimes there are, if you fly a long distance.

Yau₂ *shi₁ yau₂, fei¹ hui³ uen₂ ke⁹ tei₃ fong¹ tsau₃ yau₂.

有 時 有, 飛 去 遠 嘅 地 方 就 有

7 Is Shanghai far from here?

Hui³ sheung₃ hoi² uen₂ m₁ uen₂ ni¹?

去 上 海 遠 唔 遠 呢

8 Three days by water.

Saam¹ yat₄ shui² lo₃. 三 月 水 路

9 The engines of aeroplanes often go wrong.

Fei¹ kei¹ kei¹ hei³ shi₁ shi₁ waai₃.

飛 機 機 器 時 時 壞

10 That is certainly so, but very seldom.

Koh² ti¹ yat⁴ ting₃ yau₂, taan₃ hai₃ ho² shiu².

个 啲 一 定 有, 但 係 好 少

11 I often hear people say they are out of order.

Ngoh₂ shi₁ shi₁ t'eng¹ yan₁ kong² wa₃ yau¹₂ waai₃.

我 時 時 聽 人 講 話 有 壞

12 Yes, sometimes when the steering apparatus is not properly controlled it causes damage.

Hai, ke³, yau₂ shi₁ paai² mei₂ m₁ ho² tsau₃ yau₂.

係 嘅, 有 時 擺 尾 唔 好 就 有

THE FORTIETH LESSON

第 四 十 課—Tai₃ sz³ shap₄ foh³

1	緊	Kan²—*Important, tight*	6	穩	Wan²—*Safe*
2	急	Kap⁴—*Urgent, haste*	7	覺	Kok₀—*Realize, feel*
3	極	Kik₄—*Extreme*	8	不	Pat⁴—*Not*
4	太	T'aai³—*Too*	9	能	Nang₁—*Able*
5	驚	Keng¹—*Fear, afraid*	10	嘥	Saai⁵—*All* Saai¹—*Waste*

1 呢件事好緊要. Ni¹ kin₃ sz₃ ho² kan² iu⁵.

1 This affair is very important.

2 係好急嘅唔係吖. Hai₃ ho² kap⁴ ke³ m₁ hai₃ a¹?

2 Is it very urgent?

3 係極急定咯. Hai. kik₄ kap⁴ *ting₃ lok₀.

3 Yes, certainly, extremely urgent.

4 你講得太緊要. Nei₂ kong² tak⁴ t'aai³ kan² iu³.

4 You overstate the matter.

5 你重唔驚,驚乜野呢. Nei₂ chung₃ m₁ keng¹ l keng¹ mat⁴ ye₂ ni¹?

5 Are you still not afraid? Afraid of what?

6 呢處好唔穩陣. Ni¹ shue³ ho² m₁ wan² chan₃.

6 It is very unsafe here.

7 我唔覺得有乜野. Ngoh₂ m₁ kok₀ tak⁴ yar₂ mat⁴ ye₂.

7 I do not notice anything.

8 我先頭見佢,但不覺就唔見嚟佢咯. Ngoh₂ sin¹ t'au₁ kin⁴ k'ui₂, taan₃ pat⁴ kok₀ tsau₃ m₁ kin⁵ choh² k'ui₂ lok₀!

8 I saw him a short time ago, but, without noticing it. I have lost sight of him.

9 眞係唔見佢,但係佢不能去得幾遠嘅. Chan¹ hai₃ m₁ kin⁴ k'ui₂. taan₃ hai₃ k'ui₂ pat⁴ nang₁ hui³ tak⁴ kei₂ uen₂ ke³.

9 Is he really lost? He cannot however have gone very far.

10 佢嘅野都唔見嘥. K'ui₂ ke³ ye₂ to¹ m₁ kiu³ saai³.

10 All his belongings have also disappeared.

The Fortieth Exercise—(Conversation.)

1 What is your hurry to-day ?

Kam¹ yat₁ yau₂ mat⁴ kan² kap⁴ sz₃ ni¹ ?

今 日 有 乜 緊 急 事 呢

2 I must look for an aeroplane to go to Shanghai.

Ngoh₂ iu³ wan² fei¹ kei¹ ts'oh₂ hui³ sheung, hoi².

我 要 搵 飛 機 坐 去 上 海

3 It is not very good. To ride in an aeroplane is too dangerous

M₁ ho², fei¹ kei¹ t'aai⁷ him².

唔 好, 飛 機 太 險

4 It is not very dangerous, I cannot wait as I must try to find one.

M₁ hai₃ kei² him², ngoh₂ pat⁴ nang₁ tang², tsau₃ iu³ hui³ wan². 唔係幾險,我不能等,就要去搵

5 Why are you in such a hurry ? It is extremely dangerous.

Mat⁴ kom³ kap⁴ ni¹? hai₃ kik₄ ngai₁ him² a¹.

乜 咁 急 呢, 係 極 危 險 吖

6 I am not afraid. The matter being very urgent I must go at once.

M₁ p'a³, ti¹ sz₃ kik₄ kan², tsau₃ iu³ hui³.

唔 怕, 的 事 極 緊, 就 要 去

7 Do you wish to risk your life ? Do you not want to live ? or do you want to die ?

Nei₂ m¹ seung⁷ shang¹ me¹? 你 唔 想 生 咩

8 Are you really so afraid ?

Nei₂ chan¹ hai₃ kom³ p'a³? 你 真 係 咁 怕

9 Are you really not afraid ?

Nei₂ chan¹ hai₃ m₁ p'a³? 你 真 係 唔 怕

10 Yes, I am not afraid at all.

Hai₃, ngoh₂ tsau₃ m₁ p'a³ lok₆.

係, 我 就 唔 怕 咯

THE FORTY FIRST LESSON

第 四 十 一 課—Tai₃ sz³ shap₄ yat⁴ foh³.

1	應	Ying¹—*Ought, promise.*	6	德	Tak⁴—*Virtue.*
2	當	Tong¹—*Ought.* Tong³—*Regard as, pawn.*	7	各	Kok₀—*Each, every, all.*
3	該	Koi¹—*Ought, that.*	8	家	Ka¹—*Family.*
4	守	Shau²—*Retain, preserve.*	9	規	K'wai¹—*Custom, rule, compasses.*
5	道	To,—*Principles, doctrine.*	10	矩	Kui²—*Custom, rule, (squares).*

1 人人應要勤力學野
Yan₁ yan₁ ying¹ iu⁵ k'an₁ lik₄ hok₄ ye₂

2 學野應當用心 Hok₄ ye₂ ying¹ tong¹ yung⁵ sam¹.

3 唔該你解俾我知點樣用心
M₁ koi₁ nei₂ kaai² pei² ngoh₂ chi¹ tim² ᵀyeung₃ yung₅ sam¹⁹

4 你守住章程做就得咯
Nei₂ shau² chue₅ cheung¹ ch'ing₁ tso₅, tsau₃ tak⁴ lok₀

5 先生教學生要有人道
Sin¹ shaang¹ kaau³ hok₄ shaang¹ iu³ yau₂ van₁ to₃

6 守道德就有好德行
Shau² to₃ tak⁴ tsau₃ yau₂ ho² tak⁴ hang₀.

7 唔明白道理嘅人各樣都唔知
M₁ ming₁ paak₄ to₃ lei₂ ke⁵ yan₂ kok₀ veung₁ to¹ m₁ chi¹.

8 佢講家事就好聽
K'ui₂ kong² ka¹ sz₃ tsau₃ ho² t'eng¹.

9 當你細个个陣時你母親要你守家規 Tong¹ nei₂ sai³ koh³ koh⁴ chan₃ shi₁, nei₂ mo₂ t'san¹ iu³ nei₂ shau² ka¹ k'wai¹.

10 去處處都應該守規矩
Hui³ shue⁹ shue³ to¹ ying¹ koi¹ shau² k'wai¹ kui².

1 Every one ought to study hard.

2 In learning, one ought to exercise one's mind.

3 Please explain to me how one can exercise one's mind.

4 If you keep the regulations, it will do.

5 The teacher teaches the students philanthropy.

6 If one keeps right principles one's conduct is good.

7 People who do not understand right principles know nothing.

8 He speaks about family affairs it is good to hear him.

9 When you were young your mother made you adhere to family rules.

10 Wherever you go you ought to obey the rules of the place.

The Forty-first Exercise—(Conversation.)

1 You do not look very well, do not work so hard.

Ngoh₂ t'ai² nei₂ t'aai³ san¹ foo², m₁ ho² kom³ lok₄ lik₄.

我 睇 你 太 辛 苦, 唔 好 咁 落 力

2 No, I only do what I ought to do.

M₁ hai₃, Ngoh₂ pat⁴ kwoh³ tso₃ tong¹ tso₃ ke³ kung¹.

唔 係, 我 不 過 做 當 做 嘅 工

3 I think you ought not to do so much.

Ngoh₂ wa₃ m₁ ying¹ koi¹ tso₃ kom³ toh¹.

我 話 唔 應 該 做 咁 多

4 I say I must do so much. I cannot leave it undone.

Ngoh₂ wa₃ yat⁴ ting₃ iu³ tso₃ kom³ toh¹, m₁ tso₃ m₁ tak⁴

我 話 一 定 要 做 咁 多. 唔 做 唔 得

5 Why cannot you leave it undone? (what is the necesity?)

Yau₂ mat⁴ m₁ tso₃ m₁ tak⁴ ni¹?   有 乜 唔 做 唔 得 呢

6 Virtue is man's greatest necessity.

Yan₁ chi³ kan² iu³ ke³ sz₃ hai₃ kong₂ to₃ lei₂.

人 至 緊 要 嘅 事: 係 講 道 理

7 I say you speak unreasonably.

Ngoh₂ wa₃ nei₂ kong² tak⁴ ho² mo₂ to₃ lei₂.

我 話 你 講 得 好 冇 道 理

8 You may say what you like, I think I must do it.

Nei₂ yau₂ nei₂ kong², ngoh₂ kok₃ tak⁴ hai₃ iu³ tso₃.

你 有 你 講, 我 覺 得 係 要 做

9 If your health is injured you can do nothing.

Nei₂ sheung¹ choh² ti¹ tsing¹ shan₁, kom² mat⁴ to¹ m₁ tso₃ tak⁴ a³.   你 傷 咗 啲 精 神, 咁 乜 都 唔 做 得 呀

10 I have heard people say "man is never killed by work."

Ngoh₂ t'eng¹ yan₁ kong² tso₃ kung¹ mo₂ sheung¹ sz² yan₁ ke³   我 聽 人 講, 做 工 冇 傷 死 人 嘅

11 It depends upon what work he does, out-door work is not injurious to health.   Office work is more injurious.

T'ai² mat⁴ ye₂ kung¹ a³, hai² ngoi₃ pin₃ tso₃ m₁ p'a³, se² tsz₃ chung₃ sheung¹ tak⁴ yan₁ toh¹.

睇 乜 野 工 呀, 喺 外 便 做 唔 怕, 寫 字 重 傷 得 人 多.

THE FORTY-SECOND LESSON

第 四 十 二 課—Tai$_3$ sz^3 shap$_4$ i$_3$ foh^3

1	姓	Sing^0—*Surname.*	6	辭 T'sz$_1$—*Resign, dismiss, deny.*
2	名	Meng$_1$ (meng^9)—*Name.*	7	可 Hoh^2—*Able, can, may.*
3	齊	Ts'ai$_1$—*All, even, equal*	8	所 Shoh^2—*That which,* ("Shoh^2" *is a Chinese pronoun*)
4	答	Taap$_0$—*Reply*	9	以 I$_2$—*With*
5	公	Kung^1—*Public, male.*	10	司 Sz^1—*Control, superintend, an officer*

1	先生高姓呀? Sin^1 shaang^1, ko^1 sing^3 a^3?	Sir, what is your surname? (Note in speaking to workmen one often says) Nei$_2$ sing^3 mat^4, kiu^3 mat^4 °meng$_1$ ni^1?) What is your surname and name?
2	小姓文, 名百新 Siu^2 sing^3 man$_1$, meng$_1$ paak$_0$ san^1.	My surname is Man$_1$ and my name Paak$_1$ San^1.
3	有人問你一齊慨事你點樣呢. Yau$_2$ yan$_1$ man$_2$ nei$_2$ yat^4 ts'ai$_1$ ke^3 sz$_3$ nei$_2$ tim^2 yeung$_3$ ni^1?	If one asks you all about affairs, what will you do?
4	我要答番佢. Ngoh$_2$ iu^3 taap$_0$ faan^1 k'ui$_2$.	I must answer him.
5	佢喺寫字樓有乜公事 K'ui$_2$ hai^2 se^2 tsz.lau$_1$ yau$_2$ mat^4 kung^1 sz$_5$.	In what capacity is he in the office.
6	舊時佢喺寫字樓做打字, 但係後尾俾人開辭 Kau$_4$ shi$_3$ k'ui$_2$ hai^2 se^2 tsz$_3$ lau$_1$ tso$_3$ ta^2 tsz$_5$. taan$_6$ hai$_3$ hau$_3$ mei$_2$ pei^2 yan$_1$ hoi^1 ts'z$_1$	Formerly he was in the office in the capacity of typist. But afterwards he was dismissed.
7	你可能帶佢去文先生處搵工唔呢. Nei$_2$ hoh^2 nang$_1$ taai^3 k'ui$_1$, hui^3 man$_1$ sin^1 shaang^1 shue^3 wan^2 kung^1 m$_1$ ni^1.	Can you take him to Mr. Man's place and find some work for him to do?
8	你所講都怕係好嘅. Nei$_2$ shoh^2 kong^2 to^1 p'a^3 hai$_3$ ho^2 ke^2.	What you say is also good, I think.
9	後日你可以帶佢去文先生處搵工. Hau$_3$ yat$_4$ nei$_2$ hoh^2 i$_2$ taai^3 k'ui$_2$ hui^3 man$_1$ sin^1 shaang^1 shue^3 wan^2 kung^1.	The day after to-morrow you may take him to Mr. Man's place to find some work (for him to do.)
10	佢近來冇工做所以我想搵一間公司俾工佢做. K'ui$_2$ kan$_3$ loi$_1$ mo$_2$ kung^1 tso$_3$ shoh^2 i$_2$ ngoh$_2$ seung^2 wan^2 yat^4 kaan^1 kung^1 sz^1 pei^2 kung^1 k'ui$_2$ tso$_3$.	Of late he is out of work and I therefore wish to find some company which will give him work.

The Forty-second Exercise—(Conversation.)

1 How many people are there in your office ?

Nei₂ kaan¹ se² tsz₃ lau₁ yau₂ kei² toh¹ yan₁ ni¹ ?

你 間 寫字 樓 有 幾 多 人 呢 ?

2 Altogether there are sixty people.

Kung. maai₁ yau₂ luk₄ shap₄ yan₁ a¹.

共 埋 有 六 十 人 吁

3 I heard you had dismissed ten.

Ngoh₂ man₁ tak⁴ nei₂ t'sz₁ choh² yau₂ shap₄ koh³ yan₁

我 聞 得 你 辭 咗 有 十 个 人

4 Yes, I sent off ten lately.

Hai₃. Kan₃ yat₄ ngoh₂ t'sz₁ choh² shap₄ koh³ yan₁.

係, 近 日 我 辭 咗 十 个 人

5 Why did you send so many at once ?

Tim² kaai² nei₂ yat⁴ *ts'ai₁ t'sz₁ kom³ toh³ yan₁ ni¹ ?

點 解 你 一 齊 辭 咁 多 人 呢

6 Everything is too dear, therefore I cannot employ so many.

Yeung₃ yeung₃ ye₂ t'aai³ kwai³, shoh² i₂ m₁ ts'ing² tak⁴ kon₁³ toh¹ yan₁. 樣 樣 野 太 貴, 所 以 唔 請 得 咁 多 人

7 Two or three of them are my relations, could you take them back?

Yau₂ leung₂ saan ¹koh³ hai₃ ngoh₂ ts'an¹ van₁ nei₂ hoh² i₂ ts'ing² faan¹ k'ui₂ m₁ ni¹? 有 兩 三 个 係 我 親 人 你 可 以 請 番 佢 唔 呢

8 Exchange is so uncertain that business is very difficult.

Ngan₁ shui² kom³ mɔ₂ ting₃, maai₂ maai₅ kik₄ naan₁.

銀 水 咁 冇 定, 買 賣 極 難

9 You might do what you can for me and take them on again ?

Nei₂ hoh² i₂ t'ai² ngoh₂ min₃ sheung₃ ts'ing² faan¹ k'ui₂ tak⁴ m₁ tak⁴ ni¹ ? 你 可 以 睇 我 面 上, 請 番 佢 得 唔 得 呢

10 If I take them on again, I must send away others.

Ngoh₂ hai₃ ts'ing² faan¹ k'ui₂ iu³ t'sz₁ tai₃ i₃ ti¹ yan₁.

我 係 請 番 佢, 要 辭 第 二 的 人

11 The others may not be so badly off.

Tai₃ i₃ ti¹ yan₁ p'a³ mɔ₂ kom³ naan₁ ke³.

第 二 的 人 怕 冇 咁 難 嘅

12 I must be just in my affairs.

Ngoh₂ tso₃ sz₅ to¹ iu³ kung¹ to₃ chi³ tak⁴ a¹.

我 做 事 都 要 公 道 至 得 吁

香港・澳門雙城成長經典

THE FORTY THIRD LESSON

第 四 十 三 課—Tai₃ sz³ shap₄ saam¹ foh⁸.

1	料	Liu₇—*Surmise, material, calculate.*	6	意	I³—*Idea, meaning.*

1 料 Liu₇—*Surmise, material, calculate.*

2 通 T'ung¹—*Penetrate, whole, to reach to, to open, clear.*

3 嚊 Pe₃—*Or.*

4 啱 Ngaam¹—*Exact, right.*

5 主 Chue²—*Owner, master.*

6 意 I³—*Idea, meaning.*

7 思 Sz³—*Idea, thought.*
Sz¹—*Think, consider.*

8 疑 I₁—*Doubt.*

9 材 Ts'oi₁—*Materials, qualities.*

10 必 Pit⁴—*Must, certainly.*

1 我料唔到个个人係咁好 Ngoh₂ liu₃ m₁ to⁸ koh² koh⁶ yan₁ hai₃ kom⁶ ho².

2 你真係唔通 Nei₂ chan¹ hai₃ m₁ t'ung¹.

3 唔 知你錯嚊我錯呢? M₁ chi¹ nei₂ ts'oh⁸ pe₃ ngoh₂ ts'oh⁶ ni¹?

4 我係啱定嘑,我識佢好耐 Ngoh₂ hai₃ ngaam¹ teng₃ la¹ ngoh₂ shik⁴ k'ui₂ ho² noi₃.

5 我識佢冇幾耐,係佢做主唔呢 Ngoh₂ shik⁴ k'ui₂ mo₂ kei⁴ noi₃, hai₃ k'ui₂ tso₃ chue² m₁ ni¹?

6 係,係佢做主意 Hai₃, hai₃ k'ui₂ tso₃ chue² i⁸.

7 佢有乜野意思呢 K'ui₂ yau₂ mat⁴ ye₂ i³ sz³ ni¹?

8 我思疑佢唔好心 Ngoh₂ sz¹ i₁ k'ui₂ m₁ ho² sam¹.

9 呢啲材料唔好 Ni¹ ti¹ ts'oi₁ *liu₃ m₁ ho².

10 必定係咁嘅咯 Pit⁴ ting₃ hai₃ kom² ke³ lok₆.

1 I did not think that man was so good.

2 You are certainly dull.

3 I do not know whether you are wrong or I?

4 Certainly I am right. I have known him for a long time.

5 I know him but recently. Is he the leader?

6 Yes, he decides every thing.

7 What is his idea?

8 I think he is an evil hearted man.

9 These materials are bad.

10 It must be so.

Other words for "or" are waak₄—see list after lesson 12—and teng₃ but very frequently a slight "a" sound is given between two sentences to denote "or".

The Forty-third Exercise—(Conversation.)

1 Good morning, Sir, I have not seen you for a long time.

Sin¹ shaang¹, tso² shan₁, ho² noi₃ m₁ kin³.

先生，早晨，好 耐 唔 見

2 I do not remember whether I have seen you before.

M₁ chi¹ kau₃ shi₁ yau₂ kin³ kwoh³ mo₂.

唔 知 舊 時 有 見 過 冇

3 I think you do not believe me.

Ngoh₂ koo² sin¹ shaang¹ p'a³ yau₂ sz¹ i₁ a¹.

我 估 先 生 怕 有 思 疑 吖

4 What you think is right. When did I see you?

Nei₂ koo² tak⁴ ngaam¹, ngoh₂ kei² shi₁ kin³ kwoh³ nei₂ ni¹? 你 估 得 啱，我 幾 時 見 過 你 呢.

5 Did I not see you in that new company the year before last?

Ts'in₁ *nin₁ hai² koh² kaan¹ san¹ kung¹ sz¹ m₁ hai₃ kin³ kwoh³. 前年喺个間新公司唔係見過？

6 Sorry!

Chan¹ m₁ ho² i³ sz³. 真 唔 好 意 思

7 Do not say that, it was only that you did not notice it.

M₁ ho² kom² kong², sin¹ shaang¹ pat⁴ kwoh³ m₁ tsoi₃ i³ che¹. 唔 好 咁 講，先 生 不 過 唔 在 意 嗻

8 Yes, at that time you were young and now your appearance has changed.

Hai₃ a¹, nei₂ koh² shi₁ hai₃ hau₃ shaang¹ in₅ kam¹ yau₂ koi² pin³. 係吖，你 个 時 係 後 生 現 今 有 改 變

9 Quite so. Many people say so. Some friends cannot recognize me.

Mo₂ ts'oh³, ho² toh¹ yan₁ hai₃ kom² wa₃, yau₂ p'ang₁ yau₂ m₁ shik⁴ ngoh₂.

冇 錯，好 多 人 係 咁 話，有 朋 友 唔 識 我

10 Certainly, it is so.

Pit⁴ ting₃ hai₃ yau₂ kom³ *yeung₃. 必 定 係 有 咁 樣

第 四 十 四 課—Tai₃ sz³ shap₄ sz³ foh³

1	恭	Kung¹—*Respect, congratulate.*	
2	喜	Hei²—*Glad.*	
3	歡	Foon¹—*Happy.*	
4	結	Kit₀—*Combine.*	
5	婚	Fan¹—*Marriage.*	
6	送	Sung³—*Attend, escort.*	
7	喪	Song¹—*Funeral.* Song¹—*To lose.*	
8	費	Fai³—*Expense.*	
9	謝	Tse₃—*Thank.*	
10	笑	Siu³—*Laugh.*	

1 恭字嘅意思係有禮.
Kung¹ tsz₃ ke³ i³ sz³ hais yau₂ lai₂

2 新年頭多人話恭喜你
San¹ nin₁ t'au₁ toh¹ yan₁ wa₃ kung¹ hei² nei₂.

3 有錢佬時時好歡喜.
Yau₂ *ts'in₁ lo² shi₁ shi₁ ho² foon¹ hei².

4 佢結識一个西人朋友.
K'ui₂ kit₀ shik⁴ yat⁴ koh³ sai¹ yan₁ p'ang₁ yau₂.

5 結婚係一件極歡喜嘅事 Kit₀ fan¹ hai₃ yat⁴ kin₃ kik₄ foon¹ hei² ke³ sz₃.

6 佢係去送船唔係. K'ui₂ hai₃ hui³ sung³ shuen₁ m₁ hai₃?

7 唔係 佢去送喪. M₁ hai₃, k'ui₂ hui³ sung³ song¹.

8 送船冇送喪咁費事.
Sung³ shuen₁ mo₂ sung⁴ song¹ kom³ fai³ sz₃.

9 有人送禮俾你 你要話多謝
Yau₂ yan₁ sung³ lai₂ pei² nei₂, nei₂ iu³ wa₃ toh¹ tse₃.

10 你笑佢做乜野. Nei₂ siu³ k'ui₂ tso₃ mat⁴ ye₂.

1 By respect is meant good manners.

2 In the new year " Happy New Year " is a common greeting.

3 The rich are always happy.

4 He has made acquaintance with an European.

5 Marriage is a very happy event

6 Has he gone to a ship to see a friend off ?

7 No, he has gone to attend a funeral.

8 Seeing a friend off is not so troublesome as attending a funeral.

9 When your friend makes you a present you must say " many thinks."

10 Why do you laugh at him ?

英粵通語 Cantonese for everyone —— 香港大學粵語教材（一九三一）

The Forty-fourth Exercise—(Conversation.)

1 Where are you working, Sir ?

Sin¹ shaang¹, kung¹ hei² hai' pin¹ shue' ?

先 生, 恭 喜 喺 邊 處

2 I am working in that large house.

Ngoh₂ hai² koh² kaan¹ taai₃ uk⁴ ch'ut⁴ yap₁ toh¹.

我 喺 个 間 大 尾 出 入 多

3 I have heard a wedding will take place there.

Man₁ tak⁴ koh² shue⁵ yau₂ yan₁ kit₀ fan¹.

聞 得 个 處 有 人 結 婚

4 It is true, I am going to send them a present.

Hai₃ chan¹ ke³, ngoh₂ tsau₃ hui³ sung⁵ lai₂ pei² k'ui₂.

係 真 嘅, 我 就 去 送 禮 俾 佢

5 What a happy event it is ! I am just doing the opposite.

Chan¹ yau₂ kom'⁰ hei² foon¹ ke³ sz₃ ! Ngoh₂ tsau₃ seung¹ faan² lok₀.

真 有 咁 喜 歡 嘅 事! 我 就 相 反 咯

6 What is that ? Are you going to attend a funeral ?

Tim² a¹, sung³ song¹ hai₃ ma³ ?

點 吖, 送 喪 係 嗎

7 Yes, what a troublesome thing it is !

Hai₃ lok₀, ni¹ ti' hai₃ ho² fai³ sz₃ !

係 咯, 呢 啲 係 好 費 事

8 Yes, but they are very grateful to you.

Hai₃ ke³, taan₃ k'ui₂ ho² toh¹ tse₃ nei₂.

係 嘅, 但 佢 好 多 謝 你

9 Yes, both families are grateful.

Hai₅, leung₂ ka¹ to¹ yau₂ tse₅.   係, 兩 家 都 有 謝

10 Human affairs are really funny (you congratulate your friend on his marriage whilst I attend a funeral).

Chan¹ hai₃ ngoh₂ tei₃ yan₁ sz₃ hai₃ ho² siu³

真 係 我 哋 人 事 係 好 笑

THE FORTY FIFTH LESSON

第 四 十 五. 課—Tai₃ sz³ shap₄ ng₂ foh³.

1	奇	K'ei₁—*Strange.*	6	裝	Chong¹—*Style, to pack*
2	別	Pit₄—*Distinguish, other.*	7	箱	Seung¹—*Box, case*
3	特	Tak₄—*Special, purposely.*	8	輕	Hing¹—*light*
4	種	Chung²—*Seed, kind, class* Chung³—*To plant*	9	子	Tsz² or chi²—*Son, small*
5	改	Koi²—*Change, repent*	10	毫	Ho₁—*A ten cent, piece*

1 呢喆事咁奇 你可以解得出唔呢 Ni¹ ti₁ sz₃ kom³ k'ei₁ nei₂ hoh²i₂ kaai² tak⁴ ch'ut⁴ m₁ ni¹?

2 唔可以 个的事極難分別嘅. M₁ hoh² i₂, koh² ti⁴ sz₃ kik₄ naan₁ fan¹ pit₄ ke³.

3 个喆野咁難分別係好特別唔呢 Koh² ti⁴ ye₂ kom³ naan₁ tun¹ pit₄, hai₃ ho² tak₄ pit₄ m₁ ni¹?

4 唔係好特別, 不過種數太多. M₁ hai₃ ho² tak₄ pit₄, pat⁴ kwoh³ chung² sho³ t'aai³ toh¹.

5 船期有改冇呢. Shuen₁ k'ei₁ yau₂ koi² mo₂ ni¹?

6 船期冇改你要裝定貨. Shuen₁ k'ei₁ mo₂ koi², nei₂ iu³ chong¹ ting₃ foh³.

7 係用箱裝貨唔係. Hai₃ yung₀ seung¹ chong⁴ foh³ m₁ hai₃?

8 舊時箱裝, 就用 輕箱. Kau₃ shi₁ seung¹ chong¹ tsau₃ yung₀ hing¹ seung¹

9 隻船也野日子開身呢. Chek₀ shuen₁ mat⁴ ye₂ yat₄ tsz² hoi¹ shan⁴ ni¹?

10 我買六毫子野. Ngoh₂ maai₂ luk₁ ho₁ tsz² ye₂.

1 Can you explain matters which are so strange?

2 I cannot, those things are very difficult to distinguish.

3 Being so difficult to distinguish, are those very peculiar things?

4 Not very peculiar, but there are many kinds of them.

5 Is the date of sailing changed?

6 The date of sailing is not changed, you must get the goods ready.

7 Will the goods be packed in cases?

8 Formerly we packed them in cases, so pack them in light cases.

9 When will the ship sail?

10 I bought sixty cents worth of things.

The Forty-fifth Exercise—(Conversation.)

1 Good morning, Sir. Where are you going so early ?

Tso² shan₁, sin¹ shaang¹, kom⁸ tso² hui³ pin¹ shue³ ni¹?

早晨, 先生, 咁早去邊處呢?

2 No where particular, to-day some people want me to help them to divide a property for them.

Mo₂ pin¹ shue³ hui³, kam¹ yat₄ yau₂ yan₁ iu³ ngoh₂ t'ung₁

k'ui₂ fan¹ ka¹ 冇邊處去,今日有人要我同佢分家

3 What a peculiar job it is !

Kom² tsau₃ hai₃ ho² tak₄ pit₄ ke³ sz₈ !

咁 就 係 好 特 別 嘅 事

4 Some people think it is peculiar, but I am always doing these things.

Yau₂ yan₁ kin³ hai₃ tak₄ pit₄, taan₃ ngoh₂ shi₁ shi₁ yau₂ kom² ke³ sz₃.

有 人 見 係 特 別, 但 我 時 時 有 咁 嘅 事

5 Is that so ? There are all kinds of affairs (things) in the world.

Hai₃ me¹? Ngoh₂ tei₃ yan₁ chung² chung² sz₃ to¹ yau₂

係 咩? 我 哋 人 種 種 事 都 有

6 In this case there is something peculiar.

Ni¹ kin₅ sz₃ yau₂ ti¹ tak₄ pit₄.   呢件事有啲特別

7 Why is it peculiar ?

Yau₂ mat⁴ ye₂ tak₄ pit₄ ni¹ ?   有 乜 野 特 別 呢

8 There are two brothers, one wants to change his style of dress, but the other does not.   So they wish to live separately.

Leung₂ hing¹ tai₃ yat⁴ koh⁸ iu³ koi² chong¹, yat⁴ koh⁸ m₁ koi² tsau₃ iu³ fan¹ ka¹.

兩兄弟,一个要改裝,一个唔改,就要分家

9 Is that so ? So their point is not money.   It is clothes.

Hai₃ me¹? tsau₃ m₁ kong² ho₁ tsz², hai₃ kong² shaam¹.

係 咩? 就 唔 講 毫 子, 係 講 衫

10 They will discuss money, but at the beginnig it was not so.

To¹ hai₃ kong² ho₁ tsz², taan₃ hei² *t'au₁ m₁ hai₃.

都 係 講 毫 子, 但 起 頭 唔 係

THE FORTY-SIXTH LESSON

第 四 十 六 課—Tai₃ sz³ shap₄ luk₄ foh³

1	照	Chiu¹—*According to, enlighten.*	6	雲	Wan₁—*Cloud.*
2	依	I¹—*According to, obey.*	7	怪	Kwaai³—*Strange, blame, uncanny.*
3	漸	*Tsim₃—*Gradually.*	8	雪	Suit₀ (suet₃)—*Ice, snow.*
4	風	Fung¹—*Wind, custom.*	9	然	In₁—*Thus, so, however, yes.*
5	吹	Ch'ui¹—*Blow.*	10	忽	Fat⁴—*Suddenly.*

1 照計今日咁好天，唔噲有雨落嘅 Chiu³ kai³ kam¹ yat₄ kom⁸ ho² t'in¹, m₁ ooi₂ yau₂ ue₂ lok₄ ke̎

1 According to to-day's weather, it will not rain.

2 我估照依你講係啱. Ngoh₂ koo² chiu³ i¹ nei₂ kong³ hai₃ ngaam¹·

2 I think what you say is right.

3 但係个天漸漸黑啲. Taan₃ hai₃ koh⁸ t'in¹ tsim₃ tsim₃ hak⁴ ti¹.

3 But the sky is gradually becoming darker.

4 係有風打唔係呢. Hai₃ yau₂ fung¹ ta² m¹ hai₃ ni¹?

4 Is a typhoon coming?

5 係打風唔係，我就唔知 但係風吹落好多野 Hai₃ ta² fung¹ m₁ hai₃, ngoh₂ tsau₃ m₁ chi¹, taan₃ hoi₃ fung¹ ch'ui¹ lok₄ ho² toh¹ ye₂.

5 I do not know whether a typhoon is coming, the wind, however, has blown down many things.

6 我唔見有雲. Ngoh₂ m₁ kin³ yau₂ wan₁.

6 I do not see that there are any clouds.

7 啲雲有時好奇怪. Ti¹ wan₁ yau₂ shi₁ ho² k'ei₁ kwaai³.

7 The clouds sometimes are very peculiar.

8 落雪好好睇. Lok₄ suit₀ ho² ho² t'ai².

8 When it snows it is very pretty.

9 今日我見唔自然. Kam¹ yat₄ ngoh₂ kin³ m₁ tsz₃ in₁.

9 I do not feel well to-day.

10 點解忽然間天黑呢. Tim² kaai² fat⁴ in₁ kaan¹ t'in¹ hak⁴ ni₁?

10 Why is the sky suddenly so overcast?

Suit₀ is written in place₀ of Suet lest people should read is as Su-et.

The Forty-sixth Exercise—(Conversation.)

1 To-day something has suddenly happened.

Kam¹ yat₄ yau₂ kin₃ sz₃ fat⁴ in₁ faat₀ shaang¹ hei² lai₁.

今日有件事忽然發生起嚟

2 What is it ?

Yau₂ mat⁴ ye₂ sz₃ ni¹ ?　有乜野事呢

3 You know the customs of China are constantly changing.

Nei₂ chi¹ ngoh₂ tei₃ Chung¹ kwok₀ yat₄ yat₄ koi² fung¹ hei³ a¹ ?　你知我哋中國日日改風氣吖

4 Yes, certainly; they are gradually changing, there is no way of stopping the change.

Hai₁ a¹, tsim₃ *tsim₃ koi², *ting₃ la¹, mo₂ faat₀ tsz² m₁ koi².　係吖,漸漸改定喇,冇法子唔改

5 Why is there no way of stopping the change ?

Tim² kaai² mo₂ faat₀ tsz² ni¹ ?　點解冇法子呢

6 (In Chinese the word "fung¹" has two meanings; namely, customs and wind), you said wind, winds are constantly changing,

Nei₂ to¹ wa₃ fung¹, fung¹ shi₁ shi₁ to¹ pin³ a⁵.

你都話風,風時時都變呀！

7 " Wind " is one thing, " Custom " is another.

Chui¹ fung¹ hai₃ yat⁴ kin₃ sz₃, kwok₀ fung¹ tsau₃ m₁ t'ung₁.　吹風係一件事,國風就唔同

8 What is the difference ? In the atmosphere, the winds are constantly changing, of a country, the customs are also constantly changing.

Yau₂ mat⁴ m₁ t'ung₁, t'in¹ fung¹ pin³, kwok₀ fung¹ to¹ pin³.　有乜唔同,天風變,國風都變

9 What you say is right, in winter the air is sometimes as cold as ice.

Nei₂ kong² tak⁴ yau₂ lei₂, t'in¹ laang₂ tsau₃ suit₀ kom³ tung³.　你講得有理,天冷就雪咁凍

10 When the clouds rise, the rain will soon fall.

Hai₃, yau₂ wan₁ hei², tsau₃ yau₂ ue₂ lok₄ lok₀.

係, 有雲起, 就有雨落咯

THE FORTY SEVENTH LESSON

第 四 十 七 課—Tai₅ sz³ shap₄ ts'at⁴ foh³

1	石	Shek₄—*Stone*	6	拆 Ch'aak₀ —*Demolish, tear down*
2	磚	Chuen¹—*Brick*	7	牆 Ts'eung₁—*Wall*
3	灰	Fooi¹—*Lime, mortar*	8	瓦 Nga₂—*Tiles, earthen ware*
4	泥	Nai₁—*Clay, earth*	9	漏 Lau₃ —*Leak, forget*
5	土	T'o²—*Earth, ground*	10	窗 Ch'eung¹—*Windows*

1 山上啲石係好大 Shaan¹ sheung₃ ti¹ shek₄ hai₃ ho² taai₃.

1 The rocks on the hills are very large.

2 有人起屋用石,有人用磚 Yau₂ yan₁ hei² uk⁴ yung₃ shek₄ yau₂ yan₁ yung₃ chuen¹

2 Some people build houses with stones and some with bricks.

3 用磚要用灰嚟起 Yung₃ chuen¹ iu³ yung₃ fooi¹ lai₁ hei²

3 The bricks must be joined by mortar (lime).

4 泥多灰少唔好 Nai₁ toh¹ fooi¹ shiu² m₁ ho²

4 If too much earth and too little lime is used, the mortar is bad

5 呢處啲泥土唔係好 Ni¹ shue³ ti¹ nai₁ t'o² m₁ hai₃ ho².

5 The earth here is not good.

6 呢間屋要拆至得 Ni¹ kaan¹ uk⁴ iu³ ch'aak₀ chi³ tak⁴

6 This house must be demolished.

7 係先拆牆唔係呢 Hai₃ sin¹ ch'aak₀ ts'eung₁ m₁ hai₃ ni¹?

7 Are we to take down the walls first?

8 先拆瓦後來至拆牆 Sin¹ ch'aak₀ nga₂ hau₃ loi₁ chi³ ch'aak₀ ts'eung₁

8 Take down the roof first and demolish the walls afterwards.

9 瓦爛屋就漏 Nga₂ laan₃ uk⁴ tsau₃ lau₃

9 If the tiles are broken the roof leaks.

10 窗門都要閂 Ch'eung¹ *moon₁ to¹ iu³ shaan¹

10 The windows must also be bolted.

The Forty-seventh Exercise——(Conversation.)

1 I am very busy to-day.

Kam¹ yat₄ ngoh₂ sz₃ toh¹. 今 日 我 事 多

2 Why, are you building a lot of houses ?

Mat⁴ ni¹ ? Hei² ho² toh¹ uk⁴ hai₃ m₁ hai₃ a¹ ?

乜 呢? 起 好 多 屋 係 唔 係 吖

3 Yes, I have to purchase stones, bricks, lime and tiles. Everything is difficult

Hai₃, maai₂ shek₄, maai₂ chuen¹, maai₂ fooi¹, maai₂ nga₂, yeung₃ yeung₃ mat₄ *kin₃ to¹ naan₁ tak⁴.

係,買石,買磚,買灰,買瓦,樣樣物件都難得.

4 Have you to go about everywhere to look for materials.

Iu³ leung₂ t'au₁ tsau² hui³ wan² hai₃ m₁ hai₃ ni¹ ?

要 兩 頭 走 去 搵 係 唔 係 呢

5 Yes, I have to get some good clay, demolish the old walls and make new windows.

Hai₃, ting₃ la¹, chung₃ iu³ wan² ho² nai₁ t'o², ch'aak₀ kau₁ ts'eung₁ tso₁ san¹ ch'eung¹. 係定嘅,重要搵好坭土,拆舊牆做新窗.

6 I have told you that you are so old that you should not do so much work

Ngoh₂ to¹ wa₃ nei₁ kom³ lo₂ *taai₃, m₁ ho² tso₃ kom⁸ toh¹ sz₃. 我都話你咁老大,唔好做咁多事

7 If I do not do this, what shall I have to do ?

Ngoh₂ m₁ tso₃ ni¹ ti¹, tso₃ mat⁴ ye₂ ho² ni¹ ?

我 唔 做 呢 啲, 做 乜 野 好 呢

8 Sit down a while, do not be in such a hurry. Is it not good for an old man to talk on virtue.

Ts'oh₂ ha₂ a¹! m₁ ho² kom³ kap⁴, lo₂ yan₁ hui³ kong² to, tʌk⁴ m₁ ho² me¹ ? 坐吓吖,唔好咁急 老人去講道德唔好咩

9 What morality shall I talk about ? Do you think I am a Christian?

Kong² mat⁴ to₂ tak⁴, nei₂ koo² ngoh₂ hai₃ yap₄ kaau³ me¹ ? 講 乜 道 德, 你 估 我 係 入 教 咩.

10 Why is it not good to become a Christian. A Christian may always talk on virtue.

Tsau₃ yap₄ kaau³ yau₁ mat⁴ m₁ ho², hoh² i₂ shi₁ shi₁ kong² to₂ tak⁴.

就 入 教 有 乜 唔 好 可 以 時 時 講 道 德

11 I still want to earn money.

Ngoh₂ chung₃ iu³ wan² *ts'in₁. 我 重 要 搵 錢

12 Why do you want to earn money? It is useless to leave money to your children, your children are all grown up, and can make money

Wan² ts'in₁ tso₁ mat⁴ ye₂, pei² tsai² nui₂ mo₂ yung₃, nei₂ ke³ tsai² nui₂ koh³ koh³ to¹ taai₃, koh³ koh³ to¹ ooi₂ wan² ts'in₁ lok₀.

搵錢做乜野 俾仔女冇用你嘅仔女个个都大,个个都噲搵錢略

THE FORTY-EIGHTH LESSON

第 四 十 八 課—Tai₃ sz³ shap₄ paat₀ foh³

1	夠	Kau³—*Enough.*	6	肯	Hang²—*Consent.*
2	本	Poon²—*Root, origin, capital.*	7	爭	Chaang¹—*Strive.*
3	位	Wai₃ or Wai⁷—*Seat, position.*	8	執	Chap⁴—*Pick up.*
4	蝕	Shit₄—*Lose.*	9	反	Faan²—*Back, oppose*
5	賺	Chaan₃—*Gain.*	10	對	Tui³—*Opposite, a pair.*

1 做呢啲生意夠做唔夠做呢
'Tso₃ ni¹ ti¹ shaang¹ i³ kau³ tso₁ m₁ kau³ tso₃ ni¹?

1 Is this business a profitable one?

2 本錢多可以夠，本少就唔夠
Poon² tsin₁ toh¹ hoh² i₂ kau³, poon² shiu² tsau₃ m₁ kau³.

2 If we have enough capital it is profitable, with small capital it is not.

3 呢處地位好 Ni¹ shue³ tei₃ wai₃ ho² (a³).

3 This is a good position (for business).

4 好就好，但係做生意要蝕本
Ho² tsau₃ ho², taan₃ hai₃ tso₃ shaang¹ i³ iu³ shit₄ poon².

4 Although this is a good place yet we lose money.

5 我估你有錢賺 Ngoh₂ koo² nei₂ yau₂ ts'in₁ chaan₃.

5 I think you are making money.

6 工人肯做工就有錢賺唔肯做就冇工俾佢做。 Kung¹ yan₁ hang² tso₃ kung₁ tsau₃ yau₂ *ts'in₁ chaan₃ m₁ hang² tso₃ tsau₃ mo₂ kung¹ pei² k'ui₂ tso₃.

6 If work-men are willing to work we can earn money, otherwise they will lose their job.

7 點解你同佢哋爭 Tim² kaai² nei₂ t'ung₁ k'ui₂ tei₃ chaang¹.

7 Why do you quarrel with them.

8 佢哋樣樣都執我嘅 K'ui₂ tei₃ yeung₃ yeung₃ to¹ chap⁴ ngoh₂ ke³.

8 They pick quarrels with me in everything.

9 个啲人好反骨嘅 Koh² ti¹ yan₁ ho² faan² kwat⁴ ke³.

9 Those people are very quarrelsome.

10 時時都話反對東家 Shi₁ shi₁ to⁴ wa₃ faan² tui³ tung₁ ka¹.

10 They always talk about opposing their employers

The Forty-eighth Exercise—(Conversation.)

1 It is hard to carry on business.

Tso₃ shaang¹ i³ chan¹ hai₃ naan₁ 做生意真係難

2 Why do you say that? Being so large a firm as you are, what difficulties have you got.

Tim² kaai² wa₃ naan₁, nei₂ kom³ taai₃ shaang¹ i³ yau₂ mat⁴ naan₃ shue³ ni¹?

點解話難, 你咁大生意, 有乜難處呢.

3 You say it is not hard, I am always thinking of making money.

Chung₂ wa₇ m₁ *naan₁, sheng₁ yat₄ iu° hui⁶ wan² *ts'in₁

重 話 唔 難, 成 日 要 去 搵 錢

4 Why do you wish to raise money?

Wan² *ts'in₁ tso₅ mat⁴ ye₂? 搵錢做乜野.

5 The capital being insufficient is it not necessary for me to procure more money?

M₁ kau³ poon² m₁ hai₃ iu³ wan² me¹?

唔 夠 本 唔 係 要 搵 咩.

6 Your business is so large, why do you still wish to procure more capital.

Nei₂ shaang¹ i⁵ kom³ taai₃, chung₃ wan² poon² ts'in₁ tso₃ mat⁴ ye₂?

你 生 意 咁 大, 重 搵 本 錢 做 乜 野.

7 I have to develop my business.

Iu³ tso₃ taai₃ ti¹ chi⁵ tak⁴ (a³) 婆做大啲至得.

8 Do you wish to carry on business as big as the world?

Nei₂ seung² tso₃ t'in¹ ha₅ kom³ taai₃ shaang¹ i° me¹?

你 想 做 天 下 咁 大 生 意 咩.

9 Why not? only I fear I cannot achieve it.

Yau₂ mat⁴ m₁ seung², chi³ p'a³ tso₃ m₁ to°

有 乜 唔 想 至 怕 做 唔 到.

10 When carrying on so big a business, many people would oppose you, they would not be willing for you to earn so much money exclusively.

Tso₃ kom³ taai₅ p'a³ ho² toh¹ yan₁ faan² tui³ nei₂, k'ui₂ tei₃ m₁ hang² pei² nei₂ yat⁴ koh³ yan₁ chaan₃ kom⁵ toh¹

做咁大怕好多人反對你, 佢哋唔肯俾你一个人賺咁多

11 How could they hinder me?

Yau₂ mat⁴ m₁ pei² ni¹? 有 乜 唔 俾 呢

12 You see; So many people quarrel, affairs will change for the worse

Nei₂ t'aai² ha₃, toh³ yan₁ chaang¹ chap⁴, tsau₂ pin² tak⁴ m₁ ho²

你 睇 吓, 多 人 爭 執, 就 變 得 唔 好.

Me¹ is a very common interrogative ending.

THE FORTY-NINTH LESSON

第 四 十 九 課—Tai₃ sz³ shap₄ kaau² foh³

1	收	Shau¹—*Receive, collect*		
2	租	Tso¹—*Rent*		
3	單	Taan¹—*Account, bill, receipt*		
4	轉	Chuen²—*Revolve* Chuen³—*Turn, over*		
5	交	Kaau¹—*Intercourse, give, pay*		

6	擔	Taam¹ or taan—*Undertake, carry, a load*
7	保	Po²—*Protect, guarantee*
8	信	Sun³—*Letter, believe, faithful*
9	欠	Him³—*To owe*
10	還	Waan₁—*Return, repay*

1 佢嚟問收乜野. K'ui₂ lai¹ man₅ shau¹ mat⁴ ye₂
    1 What did they come to collect?

2 佢嚟問收租. K'ui₂ lai₁ man₃ shau¹ tso¹.
    2 They came to collect the rent.

3 我租佢嘅屋, 佢做屋主, 點解唔俾租單我. Ngoh₂ tso¹ k'ui₂ ke³ uk, k'ui₂ tso₃ uk chue², tim² kaai² m₁ pei² tso¹ taan¹ ngoh₂?
    3 I rent his house, he is the landlord, why does he not give me the rent receipt?

4 佢話你轉租過別人. K'ui₂ wa₃ nei₂ chuen² tso¹ kwoh³ pit₄ yan₁.
    4 He says that you sublet to another person.

5 我个个月都有租交, 屋主不能打理我轉租過別人. Ngoh₂ koh³ koh³ uet₄ to¹ yau₂ tso¹ kaau¹, uk⁴ chue² pat⁴ nang₁ ta² lei₂ ngoh₂ chuen² tso¹ kwoh³ pit₄ yan₁.
    5 I pay my rent every month. The landlord cannot interfere with if I sublet the house.

6 邊个同你擔租呢. Pin¹ koh³ t'ung₁ nei₂ taam¹ tso¹ ni¹?
    6 Who guarantees the rent for you?

7 冇人擔租嘅, 但係屋主想我搵人擔保. Mo₂ yan₁ taam⁴ tso¹ ke³, taan hai₃ uk chue² seung² ngoh₂ wan² yan₁ taam¹ po².
    7 Nobody guarantees the rent for me, but the landlord wants me to find a guarantor.

8 今日屋主寫擔保信嚟 問你幾時至交租 Kam¹ yat₄ uk⁴ chue² se² taam¹ po² sun³ lai₁, man₁ nei₂ kei² shi₁ chi₃ kaau¹ tso¹.
    8 To-day the landlord sent you a registered letter asking you when you will pay the rent.

9 欠佢个半月租 使乜叫緊要吖 Him³ k'ui₂ koh³ poon² uet₄ tso¹ shai² mat⁴ kom³ kan² iu a¹.
    9 I owe him one and a half month's rent, why need he be so pressing?

10 你估我欠錢冇還咩. Nei₂ koo² ngoh₂ him³ ts'in₁ mo₁ waan₁ me¹.
    10 Do you think that I will not pay my debts.

The Forty-ninth Exercise—(Conversation.)

1 It is very hard to collect rents.

Shau¹ tso¹ chan¹ hai₃ naan₁ lok₀   收租真係難略

2 Why is it hard, (to collect rents)?

Yau₂ mat⁴ ye₂ naan₁ ni¹?   有乜野難呢?

3 The landlord wants the rent, and the tenant has no money, what shall I do?

Uk⁴ chue²iu³*ts'in₁, tso¹ uk⁴ti¹yan₁ mo₂*ts'in₁, nei₂ wa₃ tim² tso₃ ho² ni¹?   屋主要錢,租屋的人冇錢,你話點做好呢?

4 You must ask him to find some one to guarantee his rent.

Iu³ k'ui₂ wan² yan₁ taam¹ po² chi° tak⁴   要佢搵人担保至得.

5 The tenants do whatever they like.   Some sublet the houses whilst some always pay the rents in arrear.

Koh²ti¹tso¹uk⁴ke³yan₁, mat⁴ye₂to¹yau₂tak⁴tso₃, yau₂ ti¹ chuen²tso¹kwoh³yan₁, yau₂ti¹shi₁ shi₁ him³ tso¹.
個的租屋嘅人,乜野都有得做,有嘅轉租過人,有的時時欠租

6 If you make them pay the rents in advance you will have no more trouble.

Nei₂ iu³ k'ui₂ shi₁ shi₁ kaau¹ sheung₅ k'ei₁ tso¹, m₁ hai₃ tsau₃ mo₂ sz₃ lok₀?   你要佢時時交上期租,唔係就冇事略

7 They will not do that.   If I send them letters they refuse to receive them (letters) If I give them the accounts they have no money to settle them.

K'ui₂m₁ hang²a³, kaau¹ sun²k'ui₂, m₁ shau¹, kaau¹taan¹ k'ui₂mo₂*ngan₁   佢唔肯呀,交信佢唔收交單佢冇銀.

8 It will not do, when will they pay up the outstanding rents?

Kom' m₁ tso₃ tak⁴, k'ui₂ kei² *shi₁ chi³ waan₃ kau₃ ti¹ kau₃ tso¹ ni¹?   咁唔做得,佢幾時至還夠的舊租呢.

9 Well, most of them will pay, but they will not pay when the rents are due.

Kom', yau₂ toh¹ sho⁵ to¹ hang² pei², pat⁴ kwoh⁵ hai₃ m₁ i¹ k'ei₁   咁,有多數都肯俾,不過係唔依期.

10 This is better, or I would not stand it (any longer.)

Kom' tsau ho² ti¹, m₁ hai, ngoh₃ yat⁴ teng₃ m₁ hang².
咁 就 好 啲, 唔 係, 我 一 定 唔 肯.

THE FIFTIETH LESSON

第 五 十 課—Tai₃ ng₂ shap₄ foh³

1	富	Foo⁸—*Rich*		
2	窮	K'ung₁—*Poor, poverty*		
3	賭	To²—*Gamble*		
4	害	Hoi₃—*Injure, harmful*		
5	呃	Ngaak⁴—*Deceive, cheat*		

6	贏	Yeng₁—*Win*
7	輸	Shue¹—*Lose*
8	求	K'au₁—*Seek, ask, pray*
9	借	Tse³—*Lend, borrow*
10	欵	Foon²—*Funds, money*

1 一个人有好多錢就係富
Yat koh³ yan₁ yau₂ ho² toh¹ tsin₁ tsau₃ hai₃ foo³.

2 點解佢窮得咁緊要吖?
Tim² kaai² k'ui₂ k'ung₁ tak⁴ kom³ kan² iu³ a¹.

3 佢時時都賭,一有錢就賭 點得 唔窮呢? K'ui₂ shi₁ shi₁ to¹ to², yat⁴ yau₂ tsin₁ tsau₃ to², tim² tak⁴ m₁ k'ung₁ ni¹?

4 賭錢真係害人咯. To² ˙tsin₁ chan¹ hai hoi, yan₁ lok₀.

5 賭錢多數係呃人嘅 To² tsin₁ toh¹ sho³ hai₃ ngaak⁴ yan₁ ke⁸.

6 佢昨日贏咗一千三百銀
K'ui₂ tsok₄ yat₄ yeng₁ choh² yat⁴ ts'in¹ saa'n¹ paak₀ ngan₁.

7 今日佢輸番一千七百銀
Kam¹ yat₄ k'ui₂ shue¹ faan¹ yat⁴ ts'in¹ ts'at⁴ paak₀ ngan₁.

8 有錢个時佢唔求人.
Yau₂ *ts'in₁ koh² shi₁ k'ui₂ m₁ k'au₁ yan₁.

9 賭輸咗,佢嚟搵求我借錢 To² shue¹ choh², k'ui₂ ooi₂ lai₁ k'au₁ ngoh₂ tse³ *ts'in₁.⁴

10 佢欠人借款不少. K'ui₂ him³ yan₁ tse³ foon² pat⁴ shiu².

1 When a man has a great amount of money, then he is rich.

2 Why is he so extremely poor?

3 He always gambles, directly he has money he gambles, how can he avoid poverty.

4 Gambling really is injurious to people.

5 Gambling is mostly cheating people.

6 Yesterday he won 1300 dollars.

7 To-day he lost 1700 dollars again.

8 When he has money, he does not ask people (for it).

9 When he loses he will come to me to borrow money.

10 He owes a great deal of money that he has borrowed.

英粵通語 Cantonese for everyone ——香港大學粵語教材（一九三一）

The Fiftieth Exercise—(Conversation.)

1 Why do some people like to gamble so much ?

Tini² kaai² yau₂ ti¹ yan₁ kom³ chung¹ i³ to² *ts'in₁ ni¹?

點 解 有 的 人 咁 中 意 賭 錢 呢?

2 Because they want to win money.

† Yan¹ wai₃ k'ui₂ seung² yeng₁ *ts'in₁

因 為 佢 想 贏 錢

3 What if they cannot win ?

K'ui₂ yeng₁ m₁ to² tsau₃ tim² *yeung₁ ni¹?

佢 贏 唔 倒 就 點 樣 呢?

4 If they do not win, they lose.

Yeng₁ m₁ to² tsau₃ hai₃ shue¹ 贏 唔 倒 就 係 輸

5 If they lose a large amount, what then ?

Shue¹ tak⁴ toh¹ ooi₂ tim² *yeung₃ ni¹?

輸 得 多 噲 點 樣 呢?

6 If they lose a lot they become poor.

Shue¹ tak⁴ toh¹ ooi₂ k'ung₁ 輸 得 多 噲 窮.

7 Well is not gambling a great evil ?

Koni² *yeung₃ to² *ts'in₁ m₁ hai₃ ho² taai₃ hoi₁ ke³?

咁 樣, 賭 錢 唔 係 好 大 害 嘅

8 Certainly it is a great evil.

Tsz₃ in₁ hai₃ ho² taai₁ hoi 自 然 係 好 大 害.

9 He owes a lot of money to the gambling ship.

K'ui₁ him¹ hoi¹ to² ke³ yan₁ ho² toh¹ tse⁵ foon²

佢 欠 開 賭 嘅 人 好 多 借 款

10 I say that gambling is very injurious.

Ngoh₂ wa₃ to² *ts'in₁ hai₃ hoi₃ yan₁ ho² kan² iu³ a¹.

我 話 賭 錢 係 害 人 好 緊 要 吖.

† Because, see separate list. Yan¹ wai₃

THE FIFTY-FIRST LESSON

第 五 十 一 課—Tai₃ ng₂ shap₄ yat⁴ foh⁵

1	世	Shai³—*The world.*	6	俗	Tsuk₄—*Common.*
2	界	Kaai³—*Boundary, territory.*	7	省	Shaang²—*A province.* Sing²—*To examine, watch*
3	限	Haan₃—*Limit.*	8	城	*Shing₁—*A city.*
4	鄉	Heung¹—*Village, country.*	9	市	Shi₂—*A market.*
5	村	Ts'uen¹—*Village.*	10	店	Tim³—*A shop.*

---

1. 自出世至到死叫做一世
Tsz₃ ch'ut⁴ shai³ chi³ to³ sz² kiu³ tso₃ yat⁴ shai³.

2. 世界有好多國. Shai³ kaai³ yau₂ ho² toh¹ kwok₀.

3. 世界大國有限,至多不過二三十个. Shai³ kaai³ taai₃ kwok₀ yau₂ haan₃, chi³ toh¹ pat⁴ kwoh³ i₃ saam¹ shap₄ koh³.

4. 有人住鄉間. Yau₂ yan₁ chue₃ heung¹ kaan¹.

5. 鄉間有人叫做鄉村.
Heung¹ kaan¹ yau₂ yan₁ kiu³ tso₃ heung¹ ts'uen¹.

6. 各處鄉村有各處嘅風俗
Kok₀ shue³ heung¹ ts'uen¹ yau₂ kok₀ shue³ ke³ fung¹ tsuk₄.

7. 中國有二十幾省. Chung¹ kwok₀ yau₂ i₃ shap₄ kei² shaang².

8. 每省都有省城. Mooi₂ shaang² to¹ yau₂ shaang² shing₁

9. 大城多數有街市,去街市買食物. Taai₃ shing₁ toh¹ sho⁵ yau₂ kaai¹ shi₂, hui³ kaai¹ shi₂ maai₂ shik₄ mat₄.

10. 喺城有好多酒店. Hai² shing₁ yau₂ ho² toh¹ tsau² tim³.

---

1. From the time of one's birth to one's death is called a generation.

2. There are many countries in the world.

3. The large countries are not many, only 20 or 30.

4. Some people live in villages.

5. The country places are called villages.

6. There are different customs in different villages.

7. There are more than twenty provinces in China.

8. There is a provincial city in each province.

9. In large cities there are mostly market places, people go to them to buy food.

10. There are many wine shops in cities.

英粵通語 Cantonese for everyone ——香港大學粵語教材（一九三一）

The Fifty-first Exercise—(On Customs.)

There are many countries in the world.
Shai^3 kaai^3 yau$_2$ ho^2 toh^1 kwok$_0$
世 界 有 好 多 國.

Each country has its boundary.
Kok$_0$ kwok$_0$ to^1 yau$_2$ kwok$_0$ kaai^3.
各 國 都 有 國 界.

In the nation there are villages.
Kwok$_0$ noi$_3$ yau$_2$ heung^1 ts'uen^1
國 內 有 鄉 村.

and markets
Yau$_2$ shing$_1$ shi$_2$
有 城 市

Sometimes the customs of villages,
Yau$_2$ shi$_1$ heung^1 ts'uen^1 ke^3 fung^1 tsuk$_4$
有 時 鄉 村 嘅 風 俗.

and those of the cities and markets,
T'ung$_1$ shing$_1$ shi$_2$ ke^3 fung^1 tsuk$_4$
同 城 市 嘅 風 俗

are very different,
yau$_2$ ho^2 taai$_3$ fan^1 pit$_4$
有 好 大 分 別

Once I went to Canton.
Ngoh$_2$ yau$_2$ yat^1 ooi$_1$ hui^3 shaang^2 shing$_1$
我 有 一 囘 去 省 城

and lived in a hotel,
hai^2 yat^4 kaan^1 tsau^2 tim^5 chue$_3$
喺 一 間 酒 店 住

I saw that in taking food
Ngoh$_2$ kin$_3$ k'ui$_2$ tei$_3$ shik$_4$ faan$_3$
我 見 佢 哋 食 飯

they did not use chopsticks,
m$_1$ hai$_3$ yung$_3$ faai^3 tsz^2
唔 係 用 快 子

But used knives and forks,
Taan$_3$ hai$_3$ yung$_3$ to^1 ch'a^1
但 係 用 刀 叉

and soup spoons,
to^1 yung$_3$ t'ong^1 kang^1
都 用 湯 羹

They were different from us in every way
Yeung$_3$ yeung$_1$ m$_1$ t'ung$_1$ ngoh$_2$ tei$_3$
樣 樣 唔 同 我 哋

It was very strange,
Chan^1 hai$_3$ k'ei$_1$ kwaai^3 lok$_0$
真 係 奇 怪 咯.

THE FIFTY-SECOND LESSON.

第 五 十 二 課—Tai₃ ng₂ shap₄ i₃ foh³

1	客	Haak₀—*A guest, customer*
2	望	Mong₃—*To hope*
3	發	Faat₃—*To give out, send*
4	探	T'aam⁵—*To visit*
5	煮	Chue²—*To cook*
6	煎	Tsin¹—*To fry*
7	廚	Ch'ue₁—*A cook, kitchen*
8	卽	Tsik⁴—*At once, now*
9	燴	Ooi₃—*Stew*
10	煲	Po¹—*Boil, (in a pot)*

1 唔係家內人, 叫做客.
M₁ hai₃ ka¹ noi₃ yan₂, kiu³ tso₃ haak₀.

1 Those not of one's family are called visitors or guests.

2 佢望有好多錢賺. K'ui₂ mong₃ yau₂ ho² toh¹ ts'in₁ chaan₃

2 He hopes to make a lot of money.

3 明日出發,就發信請客
Ming₁ yat₄ ch'ut⁴ faat₀, tsau₃ faat₀ sun³ ts'eng² haak₀.

3 To-morrow he is going-away and so he is sending letters to invite guests.

4 後日噲有客嚟探我.
Hau₃ yat₄ ooi₂ yau₂ haak₀ lai₁ t'aam⁵ ngoh₂.

4 The day after to-morrow there will be guests coming to visit me.

5 係煮飯俾佢食唔係
Hai₃ chue² faan₃ pei² k'ui₂ shik₄ m₁ hai₃.

5 Will you cook rice for them (to eat).

6 飯一定有嘅 我想煎餅俾佢食
Faan₃ yat⁴ teng₃, yau₂ ke³, ngoh₂ seung² tsin¹ peng² pei² k'ui₂ shik₄.

6 Yes, certainly they will have rice, I want to make cakes for them.

7 你个廚係好熟手 好噲煮野嘅
Nei₂ koh³ ch'ue₁ hai₃ ho² shuk₄ shau², ho² ooi₂ chue² ye₂ ke³.

7 Your cook is very experienced he is good at cooking things.

8 卽時叫起手, 就有野食.
Tsik⁴ shi₁ kiu⁵ hei² shau², tsau₃ yau₂ ye₂ shik₄.

8 Directly you tell him he has things (ready) for eating.

9 佢燴雞第一好手勢.
K'ui₂ ooi₃ kai¹ tai₃ yat⁴ ho² shau² shai .

9 He is a first class man at stewing chickens,

10 係, 佢煲湯頂好手勢.
Hai₃, k'ui₂ po¹ t'ong¹ teng² ho² shau² shai₃.

10 Yes, he is very good at making soup.

The Fifty-second Exercise—(Conversation.)

1 Do you want to invite some guests?

Nei$_2$ hai. seung^2 ts'eng^2 haak$_0$ m$_1$ hai$_3$?

你 係 想 請 客 唔 係.

2 Yes, I am asking guests to-day.

Hai$_3$, ngoh$_2$ kam^1 yat$_4$ ts'eng^2 haak$_0$ 係, 我今日請客.

3 Are they specially invited?

Hai$_1$ tak$_4$ pit$_4$ ts'eng^2 haak$_0$ m$_1$ hai$_1$?

係 特 別 請 客 唔 係.

4 No, it is just ordinary rice (meal).

M$_1$ hai$_3$, hai$_3$ shik$_4$ pin$_3$ *faan$_3$ ke^3

唔 係, 係 食 便 飯 嘅.

5 How do you invite them?

Nei$_1$ tim^2 *yeung$_3$ ts'eng^2 a$^.$? 你 點 樣 請 呀.

6 If I meet them I ask them, if not I send letters to invite them.

Ngoh$_2$ kin^3 to^2 tsau$_1$ kiu^3, m$_1$ kin^3 tsau$_3$ faat$_1$ sun^3 hui^3 ts'eng^2 我見倒就叫, 唔見就發信去請.

7 What are you giving them to eat?

Yau$_2$ mat^4 ye$_2$ pei^2 k'ui$_2$ shik$_4$ ni^1 ?

有 乜 野 俾 佢 食 呢.

8 We will stew a fowl, roast some beef and have white cabbage flowers.

Yau$_2$ ooi$_3$ kai^1, shiu^1 ngau$_1$ yuk$_2$, paak$_0$ ts'oi^3 sam^1

有 燴 雞, 燒 牛 肉, 白 菜 心.

9 Will you use chopsticks or knives and forks?

Yung$_3$ faai^3 tsz^2, ting$_1$ to^1 ch'a^1 ni^1 ?

用 快 子, 定 刀 叉 呢.

10 We are not asking them to a meal, (foreign style), we will cut up the meat and use chopsticks to eat with.

Shik$_4$ faan$_3$ m$_1$ hai$_3$ tso$_0$ ts'aan^1, yung$_3$ faai^3 tsz^2 shik$_4$ faan$_3$, tsit$_0$ sai^3 ti^1 yuk$_4$

食 飯 唔 係 做 餐, 用 快 子 食 飯 切 細 的 肉.

THE FIFTY-THIRD LESSON

第 五 十 三 課—Tai₅ ng₂ shap₁ saam¹ foh⁵

1	整	Ching²—*Make, do.*	6	在	Tsoi₃—*To be in.*
2	平	P'ing₁—*Even.* P'eng₁—*Cheap.*	7	現	In₃—*Present.*
3	價	Ka³—*Price.*	8	金	Kam¹—*Gold.*
4	跌	Tit₀—*Full.*	9	低	Tai¹—*Low.*
5	值	Chik₄—*Value, worth*	10	萬	Maan₃—*10,000.*

1 近來整得各樣貨都貴
Kan₅ loi₁ ching² tak¹ kok₀ yeung₃ foh⁵ to¹ kwai³.

1 Lately the price of all goods has become very expensive.

2 想買平野頁係幾難.
Seung² maai₂ p'eng₁ ye₂ chan¹ hai₃ kei² naan₁.

2 It is very difficult to buy cheap things.

3 成本貴, 價錢自然高.
Shing₁ poon² kwai³ ka³ ts'in₁ tsz₅ in₁ ko¹.

3 If the capital cost is dear the price is certain to be high.

4 樣樣野起價 淨係麥粉跌價.
Yeung₃ yeung₃ ye₂ hei² ka₃, tsing₃ hai₅ mak₄ fan² tit₀ ka³.

4 Everything has risen in price, only oatmeal has dropped (in price).

5 一箱麥粉值六个半銀錢.
Yat⁴ seung¹ mak₄ fan² chik₄ luk₄ koh³ poon³ ngan₁ ts'in₁.

5 One case of oatmeal is worth $6.50.

6 在別處買可以平的.
Tsoi₃ pit₄ shue³ maai₂ hoh² i₂ p'eng₁ ti¹.

6 It may be bought cheaped in another place.

7 現在洋酒漸漸貴.
In₃ tsoi₃ yeung₁ tsau² tsim₅ tsim₅ kwai³.

7 Now foreign wine is gradually becoming dearer.

8 金價一日日高.
Kam¹ ka³ yat⁴ *yat₄ yat₄ ko¹

8 The price of gold is constantly rising.

9 金價高銀價一定低.
Kam¹ ka² ko³ ngan₁ ka³ yat⁴ tings tai¹.

9 If gold rises in price the price of silver is certain to fall.

10 呢啲貨值多過三萬銀, 冇要多你嘅
Ni¹ ti¹ foh⁵ chik₄ toh¹ kwoh³ saam¹ maan₃ ngan₁ mo₂ iu³ toh¹ nei₂ ke⁵.

10 These goods are worth more than $30,000 I am not asking you too much.

The Fifty-third Exercise—(Conversation.)

1 What is called (meant by) the current price? (rate for the day).

Mat⁴ ye, kiu³ tso, shi, ka³ ni¹? 乜野叫做時價呢.

2 The current price cannot be definitely settled. If it is cheap, it is cheap; if dear, dear, that is called the current price.

Shi, ka³ hai, pat⁴ nang, teng, shat, kei² toh¹ ka³ ts'in,,
taan, hai, p'eng, tsau, p'eng,, kwai³ tsau, kwai³,
kom² tsau, kiu³ tso, shi, ka³

時價係不能定實幾多價錢, 但係平就平, 貴就貴, 咁就叫做時價

3 Is the current price for business the value of gold.

Kam¹ ka' hai, shi, ka³ maai₂ maai, m, hai,

金 價 係 時 價 買 賣 唔 係.

4 Yes, dealings in silver and gold are certainly at the rate of the day, because there is no certainty about rise and fall.

Hai,, kam¹ ngau, yat⁴ teng, yau₂ shi, ka³ maai₂ maai,,
yan¹ wai, hei² tit, mo, teng,

係金銀一定有時價, 買賣, 因為起跌冇定

5 What is the present price of gold?

In, tsoi, kam¹ maai, mat⁴ ye, ka³ ni¹?

現 在 金 賣 乜 野 價 呢

6 I have not bought for a long time, I think the price is the same as before.

Ngoh₂ ho² noi, mo₂ maai,. ngoh₂ koo² chiu³ kau,
shi, yat⁴ yeung, 我好耐冇買, 我估照舊時一樣.

7 Your ideas are wrong, do you know whether the present price of gold is high or low?

Nei₂ koo² ts'oh³ choh² lok₀, nei₂ chi¹ in, tsoi, kam¹
ka³ ko¹ pei, tai¹ ni¹?

你估錯咖咯, 你知現在金價高嘑低呢.

8 Really I do not know whether it is high or low.

Kam¹ ka³ ko¹ tai¹. ngoh₂ shat, tsoi, m, chi¹

金 價 高 低, 我 實 在 唔 知.

9 How much is a 8,9 large gold coin (American $20.00)?

Yat⁴ koh³ paat₀ kau² taai, kam¹, chik, tak⁴ kei² toh¹
*ngan, ni¹? 一个八九大金值得幾多銀呢.

10 One one-two English gold piece (sovereign) is worth more than 10 dollars, one 8.9 large coin is at least worth several tens of dollars.

Yat⁴ koh³ yat⁴ i, ying¹ kam¹ to¹ chik, tak⁴ shap, kei²
koh³ ngan, *ts'in,, yat⁴ koh³ paat₀ kau² taai, kam¹,
chi³ shiu² chik, kei² shap, koh³ ngan, *ts'in,.

一个一二英金都值得十幾个銀錢, 一个八九大金, 至少值
幾十个銀錢.

香港・澳門雙城成長經典

THE FIFTY-FOURTH LESSON

第 五 十 四 課—Tai₃ ng₂ shap₄ sz⁵ foh³

1	斟 Cham¹—*Pour out, discuss*	6	賬 Cheung³— *Accounts*
2	着 Cheuk₄—*Right,* Cheuk₀—*Used for to wear*	7	帮 Pong¹—*Help, a shipment*
3	佣 Yung²— *Commission*	8	寄 Kei⁸—*Send*
4	減 Kaam²—*Reduce, subtract*	9	再 Tsoi³—*Again, further*
5	加 Ka¹—*Add, increase*	10	放 Fong³—*Release*

1 你同佢斟乜野. Nei₂ t'ung₁ k'ui₂ cham¹ mat⁴ ye₀?

1 What are you discussing with him?

2 我同佢斟着買啲洋貨. Ngoh₂ t'ung₁ k'ui₂ cham¹ cheuk₄ maai₁ ti¹ yeung₁ foh³.

2 I am discussing the purchase of some foreign goods.

3 同你賣洋貨, 你俾幾多佣呢. T'ung₁ nei₂ maai₁ yeung₁ foh³, nei₂ pei² kei² toh¹ yung² ni¹?

3 If I sell goods for you, what commission do you give?

4 薈時佢要佣太多 但係現在我想減佣 Kau₃ shi₁ k'ui₂ iu⁵ yung² t'aai³ toh¹, taan₃ hai₁ in₅ tsoi₅ ngoh₂ seung² kaam² yung²

4 Formerly he wanted too much commission, but now I want to reduce the commission.

5 咁樣嘅價錢我唔可以加多 Kom² yeung₃ ka⁵ ka⁴ ts'in₁ ngoh₂ m₁ hoh² i, ka¹ toh¹.

5 At such a price I cannot increase.

6 薈賬你都未結 呢回要現銀至得 Kau₃ cheung³ nei₂ to¹ mei₅ kit₁, ni¹ ooi₁ iu³ in₂ ngan₁ chi³ tak⁴.

6 You have not yet settled the old account, this time we must deal in cash.

7 有帮乜野貨到呢. Yau₂ pong¹ mat⁴ ye₀ foh³ to³ ni¹?

7 What shipment of goods has arrived.

8 有一大帮牛皮 由英國寄嚟. Yau₂ yat¹ taai₁ pong¹ ngau₁ p'ei₁ yau₁ ying¹ kwok₁ kei³ lai₁.

8 There is a large consignment of leather sent from England.

9 我寫信去牛皮公司 叫佢 再寄的貨嚟 Ngoh₂ sz² sun³ hui⁴ ngau₁ p'ei₁ kung¹ sz¹, kiu³ k'ui₂ tsoi³ kei³ ti¹ foh³ lai₁.

9 I have sent a letter to the leather (company) telling them to send more goods.

10 今日放假 明日至可以起貨 Kam¹ yat₄ fong⁵ ka³, meng₁ yat₄ chi³ hoh² i₂ hei² foh³.

10 To-day is a holiday, we cannot get the goods until to-morrow.

The Fifty-fourth Exercise—(On Making Money.)

1 One day there was a shipment of goods, sent from America.

Yat^1 yat$_4$ yau$_2$ yat^4 pong^1 foh^5, hai^2 mei$_2$ kwok$_0$ kei^3 lai$_1$

一 日 有 一 帮 貨, 喺 美 國 寄 嚟.

2 He had no money to buy with, he went to a money lender to borrow in advance.

K'ui$_2$ mo$_2$ *ts'in$_1$ maai$_2$, hui^2 t'ung$_1$ yat^4 koh^3 fong^3 cheung^3 yan$_1$ tse^3 chuen^2 sin^1

佢 冇 錢 買, 去 同 一 个 放 賬 人 借 轉 先.

3 The two discussed it a long time, when the matter was arranged, he used all the borrowed money to buy goods.

Leung$_2$ ka^1 cham^1 cheuk$_0$ ho^2 noi$_3$, shing$_1$ sz$_3$ hau$_3$, k'ui$_2$ tseung^1 ti^1 tse' foon^2 hui^3 maai$_2$ saai^3 foh^3

兩 家 斟 着 好 耐, 成 事 後, 佢 將 啲 借 款 去 買 晒 貨.

4 And made a lot of money. He used the money to repay people, and was free from debt.

Chaan$_3$ ho^2 toh^1 *ts'in$_1$, tseung^1 ti^1 *ts'in$_1$ waan$_1$ faan^1 pei^2 yan$_1$, mo$_2$ him^3 yan$_1$ *ts'in$_1$

賺 好 多 錢, 將 啲 錢 還 番 俾 人, 冇 欠 人 錢.

5 His business prospered continually, his capital increased and did not diminish, and afterwards he became a rich man.

K'ui$_2$ ke^3 shaang^1 i^3 yat^4 yat$_4$ yat$_4$ ho^2, poon^2 ts'in$_1$ yau$_2$ ka^1 mo$_2$ kaam^2, hau$_3$ loi$_3$ tso$_1$ yat^4 koh^3 yau$_2$ *ts'in$_1$ lo^2

佢 嘅 生 意 一 日 日 好, 本 錢 有 加 冇 減, 後 來 做 一 个 有 錢 佬.

THE FIFTY-FIFTH LESSON

第 五 十 五 課—Tai₃ ng₂ shap₄ ng₂ foh³

1	舖	*P'o¹—*A shop*
2	搬	Poon¹—*To remove, move*
3	封	Fung¹—*Close, seal up* (*classifier for letter*)
4	埋	Maai₁—*Near, come to* (*wharf*) *close*
5	號	Ho₃—*A number or name* (*of shop etc.*)
6	囘	Ooi₁—*Return, back,* *one time*
7	牌	P'aai₁—*A signboard* *notice, dominoes*
8	招	Chiu¹—*To call, invite,* *summon*
9	記	Kei³—*Record, remember,* *a sign*
10	址	Chi²—*Address, basis,* *foundation*

1. 个 間 賣 野 嘅 有 人 叫 舖 頭.
Koh² kaan¹ maai₃ ye₂ ke⁸ yau₂ yan₁ kiu³ p'o³ t'au₁.
A shop in which things are sold is called by some people a shop (p'o t'au).

2. 有 時 屋 主 要 屋 客 搬 舖
Yau₂ shi₁ uk⁴ chue² iu³ uk⁴ haak₀ poon¹ p'o³.
Sometimes a landlord requires his tenant to remove.

3. 欠 租 屋 主 噲 封 舖. Him¹ tso¹ uk⁴ chue² ooi₂ fung¹ p'o³.
If rent is owing the landlord will close the shop.

4. 朝 早 个 間 舖 閂 埋 門.
Chiu¹ tso² koh² kaan¹ p'o⁸ shaan¹ maai₁ moon₁.
In the early morning the shop door is closed.

5. 呢 間 舖 幾 多 號 呢. Ni¹ kaan¹ p'o³ kei² toh¹ ho₃ ni¹?
What is the number of this shop?

6. 个 間 舖 我 去 過 一 囘.
Koh⁴ kaan¹ p'o³ ngoh₂ hui³ kwoh⁸ yat⁴ ooi₁.
I have been to that shop once.

7. 佢 間 舖 幾 多 號 門 牌 呢？
K'ui₂ kaan¹ p'o⁸ kei² toh¹ ho₃ moon₁ p'aai₁ ni¹?
What is the number of his shop?

8. 我 唔 知 幾 多 號 門 牌 但 係 我 知 佢 嘅 招 牌 名 Ngoh₂ m₁ chi¹ kei² toh¹ ho₃ moon₁ p'aai₁ taan₃ hai₃ ngoh₂ chi¹ k'ui₂ ke⁸ chiu¹ p'aai₁ meng₁.
I do not know his number (shop) but I know his sign (board) (shop name).

9. 你 記 得 佢 嘅 電 話 幾 多 號 唔 呢
Nei₂ kei³ tak¹ k'ui₂ ke° tin₃ wa₃ kei² toh¹ ho₃ m₁ ni¹?
Can you remember his telephone number?

10. 唔 記 得 我 不 過 記 得 佢 嘅 住 址
M₁ kei³ tak⁴, ngoh₂ pat⁴ kwoh⁴ kei³ tak⁴ k'ui₂ ke⁸ chue₃ chi².
I cannot remember it. I can only remember his address. (residence).

The Fifty-fifth Exercise—(Conversation.)

1 Do you know where he has moved to?

Nei₂ chi¹ k'ui₂ poon¹ hui³ pin¹ shue³ m₁ chi¹ ni¹?

你 知 佢 搬 去 邊 處 唔 知 呢?

2 I know he has moved to that street, but do not know the number.

Ngoh₂ chi¹ k'ui₂ poon¹ hui³ koh² t'iu₁ kaai¹, taan₃ m₁ chi¹ tai₃ kei² ho₂ moon₁ p'aai₁

我知佢搬去个條街,但唔知第幾號門牌.

3 Is it not the second door on the left after you enter the street?

Yap₄ hui⁵ koh² t'iu₁ kaai¹, chuen² tsoh² pin₃ tai₃ i₃ kaan¹ hai₃ m₁ hai₃ a¹?

入去个條街,轉左便第二間係唔係吖.

4 I do not remember exactly. Once I sent a letter but it was returned, not delivered.

Ngoh₂ m₁ kei² tak⁴ chan¹, yau₂ yat⁴ ooi₁ ngoh₂ kei³ yat⁴ fung¹ sun³ hui⁵, kei³ m₁ to³, ta² ooi₁ t'au₁

我唔記得真,有一回我寄一封信去,寄唔到,打回頭

5 Has he a signboard? (lit. I do not know whether he has a signboard)

M₁ chi¹ k'ui₂ yau₂ chiu¹ p'aai₁ mo₂ ni¹?

唔 知 佢 有 招 牌 冇 呢.

6 He has a signboard, on which is written Faat Kei Ho.

Yau₂ chiu¹ p'aai₁, se² chue₃ faat₀ kei³ ho₃ saam¹ koh³ tsz₃

有 招 牌, 寫 住 發 記 號 三 个 字.

7 Now it is after 9 o'clock, I do not know what time he closes his shop.

In₃ tsoi₃ kau² tim² kei² chung¹, m₁ chi¹ k'ui₂ kei² toh¹ tim² chung¹ maai₁ p'o³ ni¹?

現在九點幾鐘,唔知佢幾多點鐘埋舖呢.

8 I think he will be closing soon.

Ngoh₂ koo² tsau₃ maai₁ p'o³ lok₃. 我估就埋舖咯

9 If you know his address, can you tell me?

Nei₂ chi¹ shat₄ k'ui₂ ke³ tei₁ chi², wa₃ ngoh₂ chi¹ tak⁴ m₁ tak⁴ ni¹? 你知寶佢嘅地址,話我知得唔得呢.

10 Yes, if I knew it I would tell you.

Tak⁴, ngoh₂ chi¹ ngoh₂ wa₃ nei₂ t'eng¹

得, 我 知 我 話 你 聽.

THE FIFTY-SIXTH LESSON

第五十六課—Tai₃ ng₂ shap₄ luk₄ foh⁸

1	和	Woh₁—*Harmony, peace*	6	失	Shat⁴—*Lost, lose.*
2	順	Shun₃—*Accord with, obey, yield.*	7	取	Ts'ui²—*To take.*
3	聯	Luen₁—*Unite, to sew.*	8	銷	Siu¹—*Finish, melt, cancel.*
4	報	Po⁷—*Report, A newspaper*	9	簽	Ts'im¹—*To sign (name).*
5	告	Ko⁸—*Inform, accuse.*	10	約	Yeuk₀—*An agreement, treaty.*

1 世界各國每每有爭執後來和好
Shai³ kaai' kok₀ kwok₀ mooi₂ mooi₂ yau₂ chaang¹ chap⁴, hau₃ loi₁ woh₁ ho²

All the nations of the world from time to time have disputes, afterwards they make peace.

2 順道理 各國可以合作.
Shun₃ to₃ lei₂ kok₀ kwok₀ hoh² i₂ hop₄ tsok₀

If they work in accordance with right principles they can work together.

3 有時兩國聯合做好多歡喜嘅事
Yau₂ shi₁ leung₂ kwok₀ luen₁ hop₄ tso₃ ho² toh¹ foon¹ hei² ke³ sz₃

Some times two countries unite and do many pleasant things.

4 一和後,就報知各國.
Yat⁴ woh₁ hau₃, tsau₂ po⁸ chi¹ kok₀ kwok₀

Directly they make peace, they report it to all the nations.

5 報知各國, 係用一張報告
Po³ chi¹ kok₀ kwok₀, hai₃ yung₂ yat⁴ cheung¹ po³ ko⁸

They inform the countries by means of a proclamation (memorandum.)

6 失和嘅事,害世界好多
Shat⁴ woh₁ ke³ sz₃, hoi₃ shai³ kaai' ho² toh¹

Breaches of the peace are very injurious to the world.

7 有時講和一國要取第二國嘅地
Yau₂ shi₁ kong² woh₁, yat⁴ kwok₀ iu⁸ ts'ui² tai₃ i₂ kwok₀ ke³ tei₅

Sometimes when they discuss peace, one country wants to take territory from the other country.

8 但係友國要取銷以前不和嘅事
Taan₃ hai₃ yau₂ kwok₀ iu⁸ ts'ui² siu¹ i₂ ts'in₁ pat⁴ woh₁ ke³ sz₃

But friendly nations must annul former matters of disharmony.

9 兩家講和要簽字. Leung₂ ka' kong² woh₁ iu⁸ ts'im¹ tsz₃

The two parties having arranged peace must sign (an agreement)

10 兩國講和簽字, 叫做簽立和約
Leung₂ kwok₀ kong² woh₁ ts'im¹ tsz₃, kiu³ tso₂ ts'im¹ laap₄ woh₁ yeuk₀

When they sign a paper after making peace, it is called a Treaty of peace:—

The Fifty-sixth Exercise—(On Harmony.)

1 Breaking the peace, is a very disagreeable affair, we must always be at peace.

Shat⁴ woh₁ ke³ sz₃ hai₃ ho² fai⁵ sz₃ ke⁵, shi₁ shi₁ to¹ hai₃ iu⁹ woh₁ ho² 失和嘅事,係好弊事嘅,時時都係要和好

2 All should unite, yesterday I bought a newspaper.

Taai₁ ka¹ luen₁ hop₄ chi³ tak⁴, tsok₄ yat₄ ngoh₂ maai₂ choh² yat⁴ cheung¹ po⁰ chi²

大家聯合至得,昨日我買咖一張報紙,

3 That paper, said that there were two brothers, the younger accused the elder saying that the elder cheated him in the family property.

Koh²cheung¹ po³ chi², maai₃ yau₂ leung₂ hing¹ tai₃ koh³ sai³ lo² ko⁸ taai₃ lo², wa₃ taai₁ lo² ngaak⁴ k'ui₂ shan¹ ka¹

个張報紙,賣有兩兄弟,个細佬告大佬,話大佬呃佢身家

4 His friend seeing that it did not look nice, told him not to do so, but to cancel the matter.

K'ui₂ ke³ p'ang₁ yau₂ t'ai² kin⁹ m₁ kwoh³ tak⁴ ngaan₂, kiu³ k'ui₂ m₁ ho² kom² tso₅, iu³ tseung¹ ni¹ kin₅ sz₈ ts'ui² siu¹

佢嘅朋友睇見唔過得眼,叫佢唔好咁做,要將呢件事取銷.

5 If not it would be a disgrace, and people would look down on them.

M₁ hai₃ ooi₂ shat⁴ lai₂ yan₁, pei² ngoi₃ yan₁ t'aai² siu²

唔 係 喻 失 禮 人, 俾 外 人 睇 小.

6 The younger brother thought it over, felt it was true, and the trouble ended.

Koh⁵ sai⁹ lo² seung² kwoh³, kok₀ tak⁴ hai₃ chan¹, tsoi₃ hau₂ mo₂ sz꜀

个 細 佬 想 過, 覺 得 係 真, 在 後 冇 事.

香港・澳門雙城成長經典

THE FIFTY-SEVENTH LESSON

第五十七課—Tai₃ ng₂ shap₄ ts'at⁴ foh³

1	益	Yik⁴—*Benefit*	6	進	Tsun³—*Proceed, receipts*
2	利	Lei₃—*Profit, interest*	7	支	Chi¹—*Pay out, expenditure*
3	息	Sik⁴—*Interest, rest*	8	存	Ts'uen₁—*Balance, remaining*
4	派	P'aai³—*To give out, pay*	9	共	Kung₃—*With, together, all*
5	清	Ts'ing¹—*Clear, close account*	10	票	Piu¹—*A ticket, document, a tender* P'iu³—*A warrant*

1 讀書好有益. Tuk₄ shue¹ ho² yau₂ yik⁴
1 Reading books is very beneficial.

2 做生意有乜利益呢. Tso shaang¹ i° yau₂ mat¹ lei₃ yik⁴ ni¹?
2 What is the benefit of doing business.

3 生意有錢聽, 就有利息分. Shaang¹ i³ yau₂ ts'in₁ chaan₃, tsau₃ yau₂ lei₃ sik⁴ fan¹.
3 If money is made in the business then interest is paid (on one's capital).

4 呢間公司一年派幾多利息呢. N₁¹ kaan¹ kung¹ sz¹ yat⁴ nin₁ p'aai³ kei² toh¹ lei₃ sik⁴ ni¹?
4 What interest does this company pay in a year.

5 有年派二分 有年派三分除清皮費至派. Yat₂ nin₁ p'aai° i₃ fan¹, yau₂ nin₁ p'aai³ saam¹ fan¹ ch'ui₁ ts'ing¹ p'ei₁ fai³ chi³ p'aai³
5 Some years it gives 2%, if business is good it pays 3%, it is paid after deducting expenses.

6 舊年成年進款大約有幾多呢. Kau₃ nin₁ shing₁ nin₁ tsun³ foon² taai₃ yeuk₃ yau₂ kei² toh¹ ni¹?
6 What was the total income last year? (approximately).

7 今日你有支銀俾佢冇. Kam¹ yat₄ nei₂ yau₂ chi¹ ngan₁ pei² k'ui₂ mo₂?
7 Have you paid him any money to-day?

8 除支外實存現銀九萬圓 Ch'ui₁ chi¹ ngoi₃ shat₄ ts'uen₁ in₃ ngan₁ kau² maan₃ uen₁.
8 After deducting expenditure, the actual balance is $90.000.

9 合共有好多現銀存. Hop₄ kung₃ yau₂ ho² toh¹ in₃ ngan₁ ts'uen₁.
9 Altogether there is a large cash balance.

10 佢係收銀人 出入多 買長行票係好啲. K'ui₂ hai₃ shau¹ ngan₁ yan₁ ch'ut⁴ yap₄ toh¹, maai₂ ch'eung₁ hang₁ p'iu³ hai₃ ho² ti¹.
10 He is a collector he goes about a great deal it is better to buy a season ticket.

The Fifty-seventh Exercise—(On Business.)

1 A friend, and I opened a food shop, since we started, I have left everything in his care.

    Ngoh₂ t'ung₁ yat⁴ koh³ p'ang₁ yau₂, tso₃ yat⁴ kaan¹ shik₄ mat₄ *p'o³, tsz₃ hoi¹ cheung¹ i₂ loi₁, ngoh₂ kaan¹ saai³ kwoh⁵ k'ui₂ ta² lei₂

    我同一个朋友，做一間食物舖自開張以來，我交過嘅佢打理

2 Every year there was a profit. During the last year or two, nominally there was a profit, but no interest was paid on capital.

    Nin₁ nin₁ to¹ yau₂ *ts'in₁ chaan₃, kan₃ ni¹ yat⁴ leung₂ nin₁ wa₃ *meng₁ yau₂ *ts'in₁ chaan₃, taan₃ hai₃ mo₂ lo₂ poon² sik⁴ p'aai³

    年年都有錢聽，近呢一兩年話名有錢聽，但係冇老本息派

3 I asked him about the accounts, he was unable to tell me. I asked him more fully.

    Ngoh₂ man₃ k'ui₂ tsun³ chi¹ sho³, k'ui₂ mo₂ kai³ hoh² i₂ wa₁ ch'ut⁴, ngoh₂ tsoi³ man₃ chan¹ k'ui₂

    我問佢進支數，佢冇計可以話出，我再問真佢

4 And he said there is not a cash left, I asked him where he had taken all the money.

    K'ui₂ wa₃ yat⁴ koh³ ts'in₁ to¹ mo₂ tak⁴ ts'uen₁, ngoh₂ man₃ k'ui₂ ning¹ saai³ ti¹ *ts'in₁ hui₃ pin¹ shue⁵

    佢話一个錢都冇得存，我問佢撜冚嗮錢去邊處

5 He said I have lost it. Seeing that it was useless to go on, I divided up with him.

    K'ui₂ wa₃ shue¹ choh², ngoh₂ kin³ kom² *yeung₃, tsoi⁵ tso₃ to¹ hai₃ mo₂ yik⁴, shoh² i₂ t'ung₁ k'ui₂ ch'aak₆ sho³

    佢話輸嘅，我見咁樣，再做都係冇益，所以同佢拆數

6 And apart from the expenses made $500.

    Ch'ui₁ ts'ing¹ p'ei₁ fai³, kung₃ chaan₃ tak⁴ ng₂ paak₆ ngan₁

    除清皮費，共聽得五百銀。

7 But he has no cash to give me, he wrote an I. O. U. promising to pay me in full at the end of this year.

    Taan₃ hai₃ k'ui₂ mo₂ in₄ *ts'in₁ pei² ngoh₂, se² faan¹ yat⁴ t'iu₁ him³ taan¹, haan₃ i₂ kam¹ *nin₁ nin₁ mei₂ waan₁ ts'ing¹

    但係佢冇現錢俾我，寫番一條欠單，限以今年年尾還清

THE FIFTY-EIGHTH LESSON

第 五 十 八 課—Tai₃ ng₂ shap₄ paat₀ foh³

1	民	Man₁—*People*		
2	港	Kong²—*A port, Hong Kong*		
3	會	Ui₃—*A meeting, society*		
4	堂	T'ong₁—*A hall, guild*		
5	接	Tsip₀—*To receive*		
6	納	Naap₁—*To pay, receive*		
7	稅	Shui⁵—*Customs, duty*		
8	關	Kwaan¹—*Customs*		
9	法	Faat₀—*A law, method*		
10	例	Lai₃—*An ordinance*		

1 一國嘅人叫做國民.
Yat⁴ kwok₀ ke⁵ yan₁ kiu³ tso₃ kwok₀ man₁.

2 香港好多中國人做生意
Heung¹ kong² ho² toh¹ chung¹ kwok₀ yan₁ tso₃ shaang¹ i³.

3 民國有國會. Man₁ kwok₀ yau₂ kwok₀ *ui₃.

4 香港教會有會堂 名叫禮拜堂
Heung¹ kong² kaau³ ui₃ yau₂ ui₃ t'ong₁, ming₁ kiu³ lai₂ paai³ t'ong₁.

5 教會接收人要問心事.
Kaau³ 'ui₃ tsip₀ shau¹ yan₁ iu³ man₃ sam¹ sz₃.

6 交息銀係納息. Kaau¹ sik⁴ ngan₁ hai₃ naap₄ sik⁴.

7 貨物要納稅. Foh³ mat₄ iu³ naap₄ shui¹.

8 係稅關收稅嘅. Hai₃ shui³ kwaan⁴ shau¹ shui⁵ ke⁵.

9 國有國法, 家有家法.
Kwok₀ yau₂ kwok₀ faat₀ ka¹ yau₂ ka¹ faat₀.

10 香港嘅例唔俾人帶酒入口.
Heung¹ kong² ke⁵ lai₃ m₁ pei² yan₁ taai³ tsau² yap₄ hau².

1 The people of a country are called citizens.

2 Many Chinese do business in Hongkong.

3 A Republic has a Council (or Senate).

4 Hongkong Churches have meeting places, also called Houses of worship.

5 When a Church receives a member, it requires to ask his views.

6 Handing over interest is paying interest

7 Duty must be paid on goods.

8 The customs house receives the duty.

9 Nations have their laws and families their rules.

10 Hongkong ordinances prohibit people from bringing wine into the port.

The Fifty-eighth Exercise—(On the Senate and the Customs.)

1 Is this the Senate House?

Ni¹ kaan¹ hai₃ kwok₀ *ui₃ m₁ hai₃?

呢 間 係 國 會 唔 係.

2 Yes, that house is the Senate (Council Chamber).

Hai,. koh² kaan¹ hai₃ kwok₀ *ui₃

係, 个 間 係 國 會.

3 Is the Senate the same as the Customs House?

Kwok₀ *ui₃ t'ung₁ shui³ kwaan¹ m₁ t'ung₁ ni¹?

國 會 同 稅 關 唔 同 呢.

4 No, the Senate is not the same as the Customs House.

M₁ t'ung₁, kwok₀ *ooi₃ m₁ t'ung₁ shui³ kwaan¹

唔 同, 國 會 唔 同 稅 關.

5 What is the difference between these two?

Kwok₀ *ui₃ t'ung₁ shui⁵ kwaan¹ yau₂ mat⁴ fan¹ pit₄ ni¹?

國 會 同 稅 關 有 乜 分 別 呢.

6 The Senate attends to the affairs of the country, the customs attends to the duties (on goods).

Kwok₀ *ui₃ hai₃ ta² lei₂ kwok₀ ka¹ ke³ sz₃, shui⁶ kwaan¹ hai₃ ta² lei₂ shau¹ shui⁵

國會係打理國家嘅事,稅關係打理收稅.

7 Citizens should pay the duty, why do some people avoid paying (smuggle).

Tso₃ kwok₀ man₁ ying¹ tong¹ naap₄ shui³, tim² kaai² yau₂ ti¹ van₁ tsau² shui⁵ ni¹?

做國民應當納稅,點解有的人走稅呢?

8 Those who smuggle, are not in accordance with the laws.

Tsau² shui⁶ koh³ ti¹ yan₁ hai₃ m₁ hop₄ faat₀ ke³

走 稅 个 的 人, 係 唔 合 法 嘅.

9 Has Hongkong an ordinance forbidding bringing wine in.?

Heung¹ kong² yau₂ ting₃ lai₃. m₁ pei² taai³ tsau² yap₄ hau² mo₂ ni¹? 香港有定例,唔俾帶酒入口冇呢.

10 Yes, tobacco also may not be brought in, if duty is paid it may be.

Yau₂, in¹ to¹ m₁ pei² taai³ vap₄ hau², naap₄ shui⁵ tsau₃ tak⁴　有,煙都唔俾帶入口,納稅就得.

香港・澳門雙城成長經典

THE FIFTY-NINTH LESSON

第 五 十 九 課—Tai₃ ng₀ shap₄ kaau² foh³

1	商	Sheung¹—*Commerce, merchant*
2	務	Mo₃—*Affairs, activities*
3	淡	Taam₃ (T'aam₂)—*Insipid, weak*
4	旺	Wong₃—*Flourishing*
5	經	King¹—*Already, past tense, a classic, the warp*
6	已	I₂—*Already*
7	紀	Kei²—*Arrange, record, a broker*
8	承	Shing₁—*Receive orders, undertake, contain*
9	辦	Paan₃—*To manage, prepare, transact*
10	妥	T'oh₂—*Safe, arrange, ready*

1 做生意人係商家. Tso₅ shaang¹ i¹ yan₁ hai₃ sheung¹ ka¹.
1 People who do business are merchants.

2 商家嘅事係商務. Sheung¹ ka¹ ke⁵ sz₃ hai₃ sheung¹ mo₃.
2 The affairs of merchants are trade (or commerce).

3 近日香港商務好淡. Kan₃ yat₄ heung¹ kong² sheung¹ mo₃ ho² taam₃.
3 Business is very weak (slack) in Hongkong lately.

4 人人想的商務旺番. Yan₁ yan₁ seung² ti¹ sheung¹ mo₃ wong₃ faan¹
4 Everyone hopes that business may prosper again.

5 但係要經過好耐時候至旺得番 Taan₂ hai₃ iu⁵ king¹ kwoh⁵ ho² noi₃ shi₁ hau₃ chi³ wong₃ tak⁴ faan¹.
5 But it will be a long time before it is prosperous again.

6 佢已經做完佢嘅工. K'ui₂ i₂ king¹ tso₃ uen₁ k'ui₂ ke° kung¹.
6 He has already finished his work.

7 經紀同人賣貨要聽佣. King¹ kei² t'ung₁ yan₁ maai₃ foh³ iu⁵ chaan₃ yung².
7 Brokers selling goods for people make commission.

8 有一間行招人承接一單工程. Yau₂ yat⁴ kaan¹ hong₁ chiu¹ yan₁ shing₁ tsip₀ yat⁴ taan¹ kung¹ ch'ing₁.
8 There is a firm calling for tenders for a piece of work.

9 有人同人做承辦人. Yau₂ yan₁ t'ung₁ yan₁ tso₅ shing₁ paan₃ yan₁.
9 Some people undertake to act as executors for others.

10 呢個買辦好妥當嘅. Ni¹ koh³ maai₂ paan₃ ho² t'oh₂ tong° ke°.
10 This compradore is very satisfactory (safe).

The Fifty-ninth Exercise—(On Losses in Business.)

1 Formerly a merchant, opened a shop.

Kau, shi₁ yau₂ yat⁴ koh³ sheung¹ yan₁ hoi¹· yat⁴
kaan¹ p'o³ *t'au₁ 舊時有一个商人，開一間舖頭.

2 to deal in foreign goods. At first it was fairly prosperous, afterwards the landlord wanted the shop.

Tso, maai₂ maai₃ yeung₁ foh⁵ ke· shaang¹ i⁵; hei²
ch'oh¹ kei² wong₅, hau₃ loi₁ uk⁴ chue² iu³ faan¹ p'o³
做買賣洋貨嘅生意，起初幾旺，後來屋主要番舖

3 He went to talk matters over with the landlord. The landlord said he must raise the rent.

K'ui₂ hui⁷ t'ung₁ uk⁴ chue² kong² sho³, uk⁴ chue² wa₃
iu³ hei² tso¹ 佢去同屋主講數，屋主話要起租.

4 because lately rates are high; seeing that it was very difficult to remove his shop.

Yan¹ wai₃ kan₁ loi₃ tei₃ shui⁵ kwai³, k'ui₂ t'ai² kin³
poon¹ p'o³· hai₁ yat⁴ kin₅ kik₄ naan₁ ke· sz₁
因爲近來地稅貴。佢睇見搬舖，係一件極難嘅事

5 he must have a suitable place, so he agreed with the landlord.

M₁ hop₄ tei₃ wai₃ m₁ tak⁴, shoh² i₂ k'ui₂ ying¹ shing₁
uk⁴ chue² 唔合地位，唔得，所以佢應承屋主.

6 After a short time, all business fell off and the brokers seeing business so poor.

Mo₂ kei² *noi₁ kok₀ hong₁ shaang¹ i⁵ to¹ taam₃. koh⁶
ti¹ king¹ kei² kin³ shaang¹ i⁵ taam₃. vap₄ sik⁴ shiu²
冇幾耐各行生意都淡，个的輕紀見生意淡·入息少

7 and their income so little, cheated him, his business was constantly losing money, and he wanted to get someone to take it over, no one was willing to carry it on.

Shoh² i₂ ngaak⁴ k'ui₂, k'ui₂ ke⁵ shaang¹ i⁵ yat⁴ lo₃
shit₄ poon², seung² wan² yan₁ ting² shau², mo₂
yan₁ hang² shing₁ paan₅
所以呃佢，佢嘅生意一路賠本，想搵人頂手，冇人肯承辦

8 He said to people, it is really very hard to do business, you put in capital, expend your energy, and yet lose, it is very disastrous.

K'ui₂ tui³ yan₁ kong², tso₃ shaang¹ i⁵ chan¹ hai₂ ho²
naan₁, lok₄ poon² ts'in₁, yung₃ tsing¹ shan₁,
chung₁ iu³ shit₄ poon², shap₄ fan¹ m₁ t'oh₃ lok₀
佢對人講，做生意眞係好難，落本錢，用精神，重要賠本，
十分唔安略.

THE SIXTIETH LESSON.

第 六 十 課—Tai₃ luk₄ shap₄ foh³

1	賊	Ts'aak₄—*Robber, thief.*	6	罪 Tsui₃—*Sin, Offence.*
2	搶	Ts'eung²—*Steal, snatch.*	7	審 Sham²—*Try a case.*
3	偷	T'au¹—*Steal.*	8	官 Kun¹—*Official.*
4	差	Ch'aai¹—*Police.*	9	監 Kaam¹—*Prison, oversee.*
5	拉	Laai¹—*Arrest.*	10	兵 Ping¹—*Soldiers.*

1 佢係賊唔係小手.
K'ui₂ hai₃ ts'aak₄ m₁ hai₃ siu² shau²

1 He is a robber not a petty thief.

2 佢搶你乜野.
k'ui₂ ts'eung² nei₂ mat⁴ ye₂?

2 What did he steal of yours?

3 唔係搶我野, 佢去我屋蹤偸野.
M₁ hai₃ ts'eung² ngoh₂ ye₂, k'ui₂ hui³ ngoh₂ uk⁴ k'et² t'au¹ ye₂

3 He did not snatch my things, he went to my house and stole things.

4 差人點知佢偸野呢.
Ch'aai¹ yan₁ tim² chi¹ k'ui₂ t'au¹ ye₂ ni'?

4 How did the police know that he stole things.

5 我聽開佢入屋, 後來我叫差人去拉佢
Ngoh₂ t'eng¹ man₁ k'ui₂ yap₄ uk⁴, hau₃ loi₁ ngoh₂ kiu³ ch'aai¹ yan₁ hui³ laai₁ k'ui₂

5 I heard him come into the house and afterwards called the police to arrest him.

6 你中意定佢有罪唔呢.
Nei₂ chung¹ i³ teng₃ k'ui₂ yau₂ tsui₃ m₁ ni¹?

6 Do you want to determine his offence.

7 我不能定佢有罪, 要審過然後可以定罪.
Ngoh₂ pat⁴ nang₁ teng₃ k'ui₂ yau₂ tsui, iu¹ sham² kwoh³ in₁ hau₃ hoh² i₁ teng₃ tsui₃

7 I cannot fix his offence, he must be tried before he is convicted.

8 官已經審過話佢有罪.
Kun¹ i₂ king¹ sham² kwoh³ wa₃ k'ui₂ yau₂ tsui₃

8 The magistrate has tried him and convicted him.

9 有罪要坐監, 有罪就放人
Yau₂ tsui₃ iu¹ ts'oh₃ kaam¹, mo₂ tsui₃ tsau₃ fong³ yan₁

9 If he is convicted he must go to prison, if he is innocent he will be released.

10 做兵去偸野, 眞係笑話略
Tso₃ ping¹ hui³ t'au¹ ye₂, chan¹ hai₃ siu° wa₃ lok₀

10 A soldier stealing things this is funny.

The Sixtieth Exercise—(A Thief.)

1 Yesterday he came to visit me, I invited him to dinner.

Tsok₄ yat₄ k'ui₂ lai₁ t'aam³ ngoh₂, ngoh₂ ts'ing² k'ui₂ shik₄ ts'aan⸲ 昨日佢嚟探我, 我請佢食餐.

2 I told him a certain matter, a few days ago, at his friend's house robbers went in and stole some things.

Ngoh₂ kong² yat⁴ kin₃ sz₃ k'ui₂ t'ing¹, k'ui₂ ke° p'ang₁ yau₂ uk⁴ k'ei², sin¹ kei² yat₄ pei² ts'aak₄ yap₄ uk⁴ t'au¹ ye₂

我講一件事佢聽, 佢嘅朋友屋踅. 先幾日俾賊入屋偸野

3 At first no one knew, afterwards he heard a sound (noise), and called out "thief" in a loud voice, Hearing him call, the thieves ran in different directions.

Sin¹ shi₁ mo₂ yan₁ chi¹, tsoi₃ hau₃ t'eng¹ man₁ vau₂ sheng¹, k'ui₂ tsau₃ taai₃ sheng¹ kiu⸲ ts'aak₄ a³, ti² ts'aak₄ t'eng¹ man₁ k'ui₂ kiu°, kok₀ vau₂ kok₀ tsau²

先時冇人知, 在後聽聞有聲, 佢就大聲叫賊呀, 的賊聽聞佢叫, 各有各走、

4 But one could not get away, he ran and shut the door, and the thief could not escape, so they blew a police whistle and shortly a policeman came and took the thief off to the police station.

Taan₃ hai₃ yau₂ yat⁴ koh³ ts'aak₄ tsau² m₁ hei², k'ui₂ tsau₃ hui³ shaan¹ moon₁, koh° ts'aak₄ mo₂ faat₀ hoh² i₂ tsau², kom² k'ui₂ tei₃ tsau₃ ch'ui¹ ngan₁ kai¹, mo₂ kei² *noi₃ yau₂ ch'aai¹ yan₁ to⸲ tseung¹ koh³ ts'aak₄ laai¹ hui⁵ ch'aai¹ koon²

但係有一个賊走唔起, 佢就去閂門, 个賊冇法可以走, 咁佢哋就吹銀雞, 有幾耐有差人到, 將个賊拉去差館.

5 Next day the case was tried, the thief would not confess, the magistrate asked him, why he was a thief, he said, he had no food to eat, he asked why do you not work, he said, he could not find work, the official seeing that he was not old, and went into houses to steal, condemned him to six months imprisonment.

Tai, i₃ yat₄ hoi¹ t'ong₁ sham², koh° ts'aak₄ m₁ ving₃ yau₂ tsui₃, kun¹ man₃ k'ui₂ tim² kaai² iu³ tso₃ ts'aak₄, k'ui₂ taap₀ wa₃ mo₂ faan₃ shik₄, kun¹ tsoi³ man₃ k'ui₂ tim² kaai² m₁ tso₃ kung¹, k'ui₂ taap₀ wan² kung¹ m₁ to², kun¹ kin³ k'ui₂ nin₁ kei² m₁ hai, lo₂, hui³ tso₃ ts'aak₄ yap₄ uk⁴ t'au¹ ye₂, teng₃ k'ui₂ yau₂ tsui₃, iu³ ts'oh₂ luk₄ koh³ net₄ kaam¹.

第二日開堂審, 个賊唔認有罪, 官問佢點解要做賊, 佢答話
冇飯食, 官再問佢點解唔做工, 佢答搵工唔倒, 官見佢年
紀唔係老, 去做賊入屋偸野, 定佢有罪, 要坐六个月監

書名：英粵通語Cantonese for everyone——香港大學粵語教材（一九三一）
系列：心一堂　香港·澳門雙城成長系列
原著：H. R. Wells 編著
主編•責任編輯：陳劍聰

出版：心一堂有限公司
通訊地址：香港九龍旺角彌敦道六一〇號荷李活商業中心十八樓〇五一〇六室
深港讀者服務中心：中國深圳市羅湖區立新路六號羅湖商業大廈負一層〇〇八室
電話號碼：(852)9027-7110
網址：publish.sunyata.cc
淘宝店地址：https://sunyata.taobao.com
微店地址：　https://weidian.com/s/1212826297
臉書：　　　https://www.facebook.com/sunyatabook
讀者論壇：　http://bbs.sunyata.cc

香港發行：香港聯合書刊物流有限公司
地址：香港新界荃灣德士古道220～248號荃灣工業中心16樓
電話號碼：(852) 2150-2100
傳真號碼：(852) 2407-3062
電郵：info@suplogistics.com.hk
網址：http://www.suplogistics.com.hk

台灣發行：秀威資訊科技股份有限公司
地址：台灣台北市內湖區瑞光路七十六巷六十五號一樓
電話號碼：+886-2-2796-3638
傳真號碼：+886-2-2796-1377
網絡書店：www.bodbooks.com.tw
心一堂台灣秀威書店讀者服務中心：
地址：台灣台北市中山區松江路二〇九號1樓
電話號碼：+886-2-2518-0207
傳真號碼：+886-2-2518-0778
網址：http://www.govbooks.com.tw

中國大陸發行　零售：深圳心一堂文化傳播有限公司
深圳地址：深圳市羅湖區立新路六號羅湖商業大廈負一層008室
電話號碼：(86)0755-82224934

版次：二零二一年三月初版，平裝

心一堂微店二維碼　　心一堂淘寶店二維碼

定價：　港幣　　　　九十八元正
　　　　新台幣　　　四百五十元正

國際書號 ISBN 978-988-8583-72-0